ZIX ZEXY ZTORIES

Zix Zexy Ztories

Curt Leviant

ISBN: 978-1-5040-8051-4

This edition published in 2022 by Open Road Integrated Media, Inc.
180 Maiden Lane
New York, NY 10038
www.openroadmedia.com

This book is dedicated
to the memory of my devoted literary agent
Jack Scovil

HELENA; OR, SANSKRIT IS SEXY TOO

I had Walter Kleinsaltz to thank for introducing me to Helena. Kleinsaltz, my former Greek professor, was also a renegade reform rabbi. Sick of the rabbinate, he slid from Hebraism to Hellenism. However, on the High Holy Days he sidled back, when a South Shore congregation needed him for its overflow crowds. In one such synagogue I saw him in the black satin sacral robe, a little feline smile on his generous pink, almost effeminate lips. Kleinsaltz didn't believe in God. "But, thank God, neither does anyone else around here," he said. And anyway, he figured, no one could sniff out such heresy over a weekend, when even marginal Jews were excited about Deity. From a theological point of view—he wasn't totally sans scruples or ideology—Kleinsaltz felt that if on the outside chance God indeed existed, He wouldn't very likely punish him for being a rascal three days a year. Hypocrisy for Kleinsaltz, like consistency for Emerson, was a hobgoblin of little minds.

A few months after I'd had my last class with him, I bumped into him on the run in the hall of the synagogue where I taught Jewish history. His robe ballooned behind him. It was the first day of Rosh Hashana and instead of shaking hands and wishing each other a good year, we spontaneously pressed our index fingers to our lips—a sign to keep mum. We'd caught each other moonlighting. As a graduate student on a $5,500-a-year stipend, I was forbidden to work (a rule made by $60,000-a-year deans); and he, as an untenured assistant professor—probably the oldest one on the Cotton Mather College campus—he too was prohibited by university regulations from accepting outside employment. Only tenured faculty members were permitted to take on extra jobs.

"Where are you running to?" I asked.

"I forgot my sermon," he panted. "I hope it's in the car."

Kleinsaltz was a bumbling teacher. He forgot his books, his notes, his facts. He said Sparta when he meant Athens. He quoted Plato, but it was Aristotle. He probably hadn't read either in years. He mixed up Oedipus and Odysseus. Once he referred to the Odyssey complex. Questioned, he said he meant the yearning for wanderlust. Menelaus came out Menelayer. He mixed up Thucydides and Herodotus, and called Aristophanes the greatest living tragedian. When the class, used to his boners and usually discreetly silent, now yelled out, "What?" he blushed and said, "If Chekhov wrote comedies and fools call Kafka's work comic, then Aristophanes wrote tragedies. Period!"

I don't know how he ever got into Cotton Mather, unless it was because he had known Professor Roman Ingelberg (the triple threat: Sanskrit, Arabic, Greek) in England, where they both settled after fleeing Nazi Germany. But Kleinsaltz covered all this up with a good-natured, self-effacing grace, his English tinged with that slight, cultivated Jewish-German accent (there is a difference between a Jew speaking German and others) that made us forgive him.

Kleinsaltz was along in years, probably in his late forties.

Being an assistant professor at forty-eight or forty-nine was like being a busboy at forty. Even waiting was hopeless.

I invited Kleinsaltz to come after services for a holiday lunch.

After the meal he inspected my three small rooms and said, "Maybe it's time you settled down?" He leaned back into my over-stuffed armchair. There was a mauve, winy glow on his cheeks.

"You don't like my cooking?" I said.

"It's delicious. You teach here?"

I pressed my finger to my lips.

"You preach here?" I countered.

He winked. "I didn't hear a word. I don't know a thing. Pass me some more of that delicious bribe. I mean brine. *Wine!* I didn't know you know Hebrew."

"I don't. That's why I teach in a reform congregation. And I didn't know you were a rabbi."

"Shh. Don't tell a soul. I graduated from a rabbinical seminary before I went into Greek. Let's have some more of that Tokay."

I poured him another glass. He said, "L'chayim," and sipped the wine happily.

"It doesn't bother you," I said, my voice rising in indignation, "that you're stuck in this dreary, water-logged Massachusetts town for two days and that the Rabbi Kahn who hired you to lead Rosh Hashana services for the once-a-year overflow crowd didn't have the Jewish decency to invite you for a holiday meal? How would he feel if the case had been reversed?"

"You mean if he were me and I were he?"

"Exactly. Wouldn't he feel rotten?" I asked.

"He'd feel terrible. I wouldn't have invited him either. Why should I invite an atheist to lunch? Would you?"

"Of course not."

We looked at each other in silence. We smiled. A look of understanding passed between us as if we'd been friends for years.

"Would you like some more meatloaf?" I said.

Chin up, his head leaning against the back of the easy chair, Kleinsaltz wagged a finger at me. "You're drunk. A man needs a helpmeet, says the Bible. No one should make loaf alone." He smiled, lips closed, a softly ironic grin. He ticked his head; it was he who was slightly drunk. "How old are you, if I may ask?"

"Twenty-nine, almost twenty-eight."

"Really? You look twenty-five. When were you in my class?"

"This past spring."

"That long ago? You looked twenty-six then."

"It runs in the family. We all look twenty-five. My father, my mother, even my sister."

"How old is she?"

"Thirteen."

"You *are* drunk. Pass the bribe. She's only thirteen?"

"Yes."

"If she looks like you, I'll wait for her. Twenty-nine? High time. I married late too. At thirty-two. Everyone thought there was no hope for me. But I've been married sixteen years now. And believe me this is the best meatloaf I've ever had. If I were ten years younger I'd fall for you."

"I can cook but I can't type."

"Liselotta can't cook but she types well. With my scholarly and research output, I need a full-fleshed typist full time at home. She wears horn-rim glasses and shoes too tight they should fit her like gloves."

The herr doctor rabbiner professor hiccupped. He covered his mouth, blushed. I uncorked another bottle of Carmel.

Kleinsaltz filled his water glass and downed it like iced tea. By now his slightly Germanic accent became more pronounced.

"There's a girl I want you to meet. . . . Your name is Keller, isn't it?" he giggled into his palm. "I like to share. I'll arrange something soon." He pressed his index finger to his lip. "Discreetly."

I didn't think he'd remember, drunk as he was, but he kept his word. One evening that rabbi manqué called from Boston to invite me to a party. I told him I'd like to come but already had a date that evening.

"No matter, bring her along for me. That girl I want you to meet is going to be there."

My date and I came into Kleinsaltz's Commonwealth Avenue apartment holding hands. Janie was tall, beautifully baby-faced, Chinese-eyed. She radiated simplicity, innocence. But seeing the three bearded professors—one had his fist raised like Demosthenes—at the far side of the oblong living room, her hand fell slack. What's Professor Ingelberg doing here? I wondered.

Kleinsaltz introduced me to his darkly homely wife and to Mrs. Ingelberg. Then a subtly European glimmer lit his eyes. "And this is Helena Ingelberg."

Helena, looking rather bored, sat primly with a blazer over her well-filled blouse, but I already felt on my skin the warmth she exuded. I looked away for a moment. In my mind's eye, I saw her strongly chiseled, pretty face and sensed the dagger-eyed vitality she radiated. I'm going to make it with Ingelberg's daughter, I knew, and blessed my luck in having wined and dined Kleinsaltz. I blessed the whole karma of our coming together at the proper time.

Finally, after a few seconds, Helena said in her tweedy

English accent, "Pleased to meet you." She leaned forward, shook my hand quickly and lightly, avoiding even the suggestion of a touch. Then, facing Janie, said: "And you too. What did you say your name was?" Her green eyes excoriated Janie with a razor glance, cutting down a rival.

"They call me Janie."

Janie looked uncomfortable. She hardly said a word. Who's gonna take this albatross home? I screamed. Janie grazed my lobe with her lips and whispered, "What are those men talking about over there? Are they singing?" I looked at the three men huddled close at the edge of three low-slung chairs, an all-male Greek chorus, full professors full of classical Greek, having a grand old time in its repressed, muted way, like bishops, I suppose, at an ecumenical convention, larding their talk with double-entendre Septuagint quotes.

I lifted up a wave of Janie's hair. The hair near her temple was moist and matted.

"They're singing the *Bhagavad Gita*," I said loud enough for Helena to hear. "It's a sort of classical Oedipal trio. They're trying to achieve cosmic yantra."

"Will you stop shouting out your answers?" Janie said behind her hand. "Everyone is looking. Why did you bring me to a professor's party? I feel so stupid here. Lord, I'm only a freshman."

"I thought that was a senior dance I picked you up at."

"I went anyway."

The party had broken up into groups. The profs, the two women, Janie and I, and Helena sitting in the love seat, unloved, leaning now toward her mother, now hesitantly toward us. Finally, Helena rose and said, "Here, Walter, let me help you clear the tables."

"Take me home," Janie whispered, her porcelain face pale.

"What am I doing at a faculty party?" Then her eyes narrowed. "They don't sound like they're singing."

"Chanting. That's the word. It's not like singing. It's *sprakhshtimeh*. One is reciting the *Bhagavad Gita* in Sanskrit. The other, the fellow with the beard like a shovel, that's Helena's daddy, he's translating it into classical Greek. The short man is translating the Greek into Arabic. What they're doing is called *nekomeh*. An Arabic marketplace rite that goes back—let's see—to the middle of the seventh, some say early eighth, century when the Sicilian scholastics under idiotic Moorish hegemony would vie for idiosyncratic prizes for idiomatic simultaneous symbiotic classical translation."

"I don't feel well," Janie said softly. She pursed her lips. Holding back tears? Good, I thought. Maybe the ambulance will take you home. "I'm only sixteen."

"What?" I roared.

Helena's mother and Mrs. Kleinsaltz gaped at me. Helena, who had just come back into the living room, also heard. For a moment, half a beat, perhaps a dactyl, the chanting broke off.

I rose and brought Janie to the kitchen part of the living/dining room.

"What?" I hissed. "I thought you were eighteen. You're making a first-class anapest of yourself. Here I take you to the only place in the world where classical fenugreek is spoken. Don't tell me you're sixteen."

"I made high school in two and a half years," Her head started to tilt back. "Get me water. Quick." Her eyes blazed in a fever. "You're mean and sly and nasty," she said. "How old are you?"

"Twenty-six. No. that's a lie. I'm thirty-nine."

"You look it."

She clapped her hand to her mouth. "And I kissed you. I want to rinse my mouth."

"Nekomeh. Sanskrit. Fez. Fawn. Fenugreek. Yantra."

"Why do you keep saying that?"

"I feel good. I like the rhythm. I like the people here. I'm having a grand time despite you."

"I never want to see you again. You're absolutely the vilest, meanest person I've ever met. You're an inconsiderate b . . . b . . . bastard." And a red flush inundated her china teacup face like a tidal wave. "You're so old"—she blushed again—"and I'm only fifteen and a half."

"You get younger by the minute. Soon we'll have to rent a stroller."

"Excuse me." She swept away, as if gathering her skirts like a heroine of a southern historical novel, and went up to Mrs. Kleinsaltz. "Where's the ladies' room? I think I'm going to pass out."

"She's been drinking like a fish," Helena said.

"Oh, I have not. I've been sipping 7-Up all evening."

Just then the men rose, signaling the end of the party. Now the women also stood. Helena too. I didn't realize how tall she was. I noticed her long, swaggly legs, her demure ass. She went to the dining room and looked at herself in the mirror. Not the shy, averted glance most people use in the mirror. She watched herself staring back, and watched me watching her. I liked looking at her in the mirror, doubling her presence.

"Quite a beautiful girl, that Janie," she told the glass, addressing me.

"You sure are."

Helena turned from the mirror. She seized me with her strong green eyes.

The door closed. Ingelberg's two colleagues departed quickly. Then came one of those moments of silence when people have run out of things to say and are dreaming up a pleasantry to carry them gracefully to the exit. The Ingelbergs and Kleinsaltzes faced each other. Then a long loud flush rattled the thin walls.

Suddenly all four began to speak. I stepped toward Helena, hoping that Janie would have a good long cry in the john.

"Do you go to school?" I asked.

"I'm at Harvard," she said in her lovely English music hall voice.

"Really?"

She waited a moment. "I'm a secretary."

The door was now open. Helena watched her father shaking hands with Kleinsaltz. Ingelberg then shook Mrs. Ingelberg's hand. "Thank you for having us." Then he took Mrs. Kleinsaltz's arm and walked out with her.

"Roman!" Mrs. Ingelberg chided.

"Oh, I'm terribly sorry," Ingelberg laughed, paunch quivering. "I took your wife by mistake."

"That's all right," Kleinsaltz consoled him. "Any time."

Professor Ingelberg walked over to me, recognizing (diplomatic lingo) me for the first time that evening. He had fat rolls on the back of his neck that reminded me of an ogrook I had once seen in Alaska. He wiggled his brows at me and said, "Don't I know you from somewhere?"

"Yes, I'm Keller. I was your student in several Sanskrit courses."

"Oh, yes. Of course. Rather bright fellow, Keller was." He seemed to muse off into the distance for a moment, then added, "What's Keller doing nowadays, do you know?"

"He's doing graduate work in your department."

"Good. Good," Ingelberg said. He pulled out a little notebook—his hefty belly was a barrier between us—and jotted down my name, address, and phone number. In the swing of things, I did the same. I glanced over to Helena who watched this game with amused skepticism.

Helena took a deep breath—I riveted my eyes on her expanding, rising chest—and tugged her blazer down.

"I work for the botany department," she said.

"I'll call you Monday morning." I said. When Janie came out, I loudly asked if anyone needed a lift, assuming that if Ingelberg didn't have a car I could drive the family home.

"Actually," he said, "I wanted to ring up a taxi."

Now Helena kissed Mrs. Kleinsaltz. She pressed up to Kleinsaltz too and kissed him. He emitted his weak, effeminate smile.

"Good night, Walter," she said.

"I'll take you home," I told Ingelberg.

"Very good of you," Ingelberg said, as more goodbyes rebounded and conversation rose to an excitement it had not attained all evening.

"Are there lectures you'd like to go to, professor?" I asked softly. "Since you don't have a car, I'll be glad to take you."

"I very rarely go to lectures that I myself don't give," he said, "and occasionally I don't even attend those."

"I'm the same way," I said. "No sense going to lectures to hear things I don't know. I want to reassure myself on the things I already know."

"Most assuredly. Most assuredly," the professor responded.

Now everyone made his way out. I watched Helena walking down the long hall. She had that self-sure stride that parted crowds and water. In the doorway Kleinsaltz touched my elbow, pulled me aside. "Keller, you make good meatloaf." He hiccupped. "Just like my mother used to make. You won my heart. My wife, poor thing," he rolled his eyes. "Just look at me. Skin and bones."

As I walked to the door, Kleinsaltz added softly, "As soon as I get my tenure, I'm going to marry her."

"Who?" Perhaps he'd already proposed to Janie.

Kleinsaltz made a little swan out of his bent wrist and closed fingertips and pointed down the hall. He was drunk, the old lecher. "Her, her. Maybe before. As soon as one becomes famous, God willing, one dumps one's wife." Kleinsaltz squeezed me familiarly above the elbow. "*Sie ist zum haben.* Provided," he winked, "you like camels with two humps."

My God, I thought, the Greek he's been teaching for two decades has seduced him. Now to his triple crown of professor, exreform rabbi, and atheist, fag followed a feckless fourth.

We drove in silence. Janie and I in front. Helena and Ingelberg and his wife—no scarecrow either—in the back. How the two of them had managed to make a lanky lovely bodied girl like Helena was beyond my ken of genes. Janie, mad as hell, stared straight ahead, as if the safety of the trip depended on it. With an occasional comment, Helena tried to keep the silence from becoming too oppressive. My only fear was that Janie might ask Ingelberg what *nekomeh* meant ("revenge" in Yiddish), or if they really had been translating the *Bhagavad Gita.*

I parked around the corner from Janie's dorm. Inside, Janie murmured, "You were talking to me, but she's really the one you came to see, isn't she? I'll bet the sparks are going to fly between you and that nasty girl."

From your mouth to God's ears, sweet prophet, I didn't say.

"Not at all. You're bright, but not bright enough. *You're* my date. I called you. I picked you up. I brought you into prestigious company the likes of which you'll never again see in your life. I taught you things you've never known and will never understand. I stood up for you when the going got rough. I sensed you going tight with fear as soon as we stepped into the apartment. You couldn't cope. A rill of quivers, ending in a sudden pre-orgasmic stiffening, ran through your arm. You became pale. Your eyes rolled . . ."

"Oh, they did not."

"Your tongue cleaved to the roof of your mouth. Looking at your angelic countenance, I wondered how it would feel to rape a cherub. I tried to give you a good time and I brought you home. Now that's about as complete a cycle as one could wish for on a date with the exception of intercourse. Now didn't you have a good time?"

"No . . . well, yes, it was kind of glittering for a while in a scary sort of way. Then you started making fun of me, just like you're doing now in that condescending sort of way," she said in a firm voice, looking me straight in the eye. "It showed me what you're really like. You put on the *front* of being a nice guy, but when the opportunity presents itself, you show your true colors."

"Kiss me," I said. "That statement, despite the string of clichés which you'll be cured of in second semester freshman English, shows me you've matured out of babyhood. Bravo."

"Please don't call me again. I'm only fifteen. You're old enough to be my father."

"Let's have those luscious lips."

"No."

"Shut up. Grow up. Pucker up."

She leaned against the wall. Closed her eyes. I brushed her baby lips lightly. "Feh. Ovaltine. Embracing you is like hugging a mirror image or wax statue. Perfect reproduction sans sniff or sense of flesh. Kissing you is like kissing a spool of thread, Nefertiti in the British Museum with a towel over her mouth."

Her eyes were still closed when I walked away.

"You're the rottenest person I ever met in my whole life.

I wish Helena takes *nekomeh* on you. We speak Yiddish at home."

Helena was already sitting in the front seat (her Jewish ma's urging), giving her parents some room in the back. I followed her instructions out to one of the fancy Boston suburbs. Driving along the Charles River and then through the nicely tree-arched streets with wide lawns and brick mansions, I fantasized I was with my wife and soon we'd go to bed and listen to crickets or whatever they listen to in the suburbs when the windows are open. Then I woke up.

I thought she'd at least hover by the door when her parents entered their stunning Tudor. But nothing doing. She left with mom and dad, their syncopated profuse thanks hanging thick in the night air like sap from a tree. I wasn't even invited in for a glass of water.

On the way home, I thought about my career and my thoughts darkened. I'd given my best years to studying. At night, dreams washed everything away, but in the morning Sanskrit Sanskrit Sanskrit rushed in like an execration. Despondence overwhelmed me. All my friends were driving Jaguars, going skiing, building empires. All I had to look forward to was a contemplative past. For a gloomy moment, I felt like a character in a Chekhov play, and the dark road and me all alone in the cherry orchard darkness didn't help my morose mood.

The only bright light—I swear it was like a bulb illuminated within me—was Helena. But her presence was so distracting, I had to concentrate on Sanskrit to give me peace. I created a concentric *bindu* for myself and wound my thoughts around and around until I relaxed. Some state of affairs, me thinking of the very thing I wanted to repress. Why did she haunt me so after one brief meeting? Because I knew no other girl who could make me forget Sanskrit, that fellowship that had run aground and would never come to shore. Too bad Plato and Maimonides and Caesar and Moses couldn't be revivified. With them I'd have opened up a quintuple classical language school so elite we wouldn't admit anyone. Maimonides for Arabic, Plato for Greek, Caesar for Latin, and Moses for Hebrew. And me, I'd be dean and hold the broken-legged Sanskrit chair.

The first time Helena and I went out we sparred at the café all evening. Where was that sexual wavelength I could have sworn we'd be on? I saw it in her eyes in Kleinsaltz's apartment, a mocking little gleam in her verdure eyes that tried to offset the natural vulnerability of the want/want/want she radiated. But in the café, where everyone sat close, where the air was steamy, the songs thick, the atmosphere cozy, Helena was cold. Maybe I was hostile because she refused me two dates in a row. I had not run into such a desirable girl in years—I had no stomach for the scarecrows and mummies who patronized grad studies in a desperate effort to undo their destined prissy spinsterhood. "What do you say we go out the next two Saturday nights?" I had asked her the first time I called. I sweated in the phone booth. The sour smell of other people's conversations clung to the mouthpiece like a sticky substance.

"I haven't even gone out with you once, why should I agree to going out twice?"

At that moment the British lilt in her voice tempted me even more.

"Twice is twice as good as once. Everyone knows that once is not enough. And, anyway, you ought to be flattered."

Now in the café, she suddenly asked me, "Have you known Walter long?"

"About two years."

"He's a character," she chuckled. "But lovable."

"And he's lots of fun," I said. "Bright. Prolific in books and writings."

Helena covered a burst of laughter, swooping hand to mouth.

"Why are you laughing?"

"Speak no evil. Walter is a friend of ours. Like our Arabist friends would say, You don't stab your host in the back, especially if he introduces you to a good-looking guy."

(The next day I ran to the Widener Library, one of the few times I entered the place. Like Kleinsaltz, I loved learning too much to spoil it by reading. Never having read anything by him, I searched out Kleinsaltz's bibliography. Technically, Kleinsaltz was right. Plurally speaking, no liar at all. Books he had. Writings too. Two slim volumes that ancient writers had written and modern ones had translated and edited. For each of which—when they had gone out of print and a new edition was needed to secure copyright—he had provided a modest two-page preface that, in inverse proportion to its importance, he lengthily labeled a prolegomenon. And one article, his two prefaces welded together, in an obscure New Zealand journal that had ceased publication with the issue he'd contributed to.)

"What do you plan to do with yourself?" Helena peered over the rim of her teacup.

"Do? I don't want to do anything."

Helena made a disapproving face.

"What can I do with Sanskrit?" I said, wondering if she was listening, or if like a magnet she was busy receiving stares directed at her like fields of force. I leaned forward, said with more drama than I felt, "Teach it in some Monday and Wednesday afternoon school to Hindi children? I can just see the matrons, all with that little crimson dot on their brown brows and fat asses that loose saris can't hide. I can just see the kids squirming in their carpools. 'Ma, I don't want to go to

Sanskrit school and I can't stand the teacher he always asks me if I say Krishna before I go to sleep.'"

Helena smiled briefly at this little Jewish joke. Her mouth was tight, to signal she wasn't vastly amused, but the sparkle in her eyes said otherwise. "You don't have a very tolerant view of people, do you?"

"Directing one's prejudices at one group is undemocratic. I spread my intolerance, thin and even."

Helena took another sip of tea and again peered over the cup at me. "Why'd you go into Sanskrit?"

"To save my life."

Helena put the cup down. Her head turned, following the members of the band leaving the stage. A flood of jealousy came over me. Then she remembered me. "Now there's an interesting twist. What is that supposed to mean? Since when is Sanskrit a lifesaver?"

"Everyone I knew was being taken to Vietnam. The army was still giving exemptions for grad students and juicy National Defense Fellowships were being offered for people studying exotic Asian languages. Defense of America, yessiree."

Helena released the brake of her amusement and now smiled full force. "Is that really how you got into Sanskrit? I can't tell now when you're fooling."

"Sure. Life above all. Keller is first in my book. To save him, I was willing to do anything, even study Sanskrit. Sanskrit is like Scotch or sex, after the first two or three you get to love it."

"Is that really true?"

"Say it again."

"But why?"

"I like the mellifluous, titillating, satiny sound of your New Bond Street voice. I like its timbre, its vibrato. I like the way your vocal cords vibrate. That crisp, lilting English tickles me where it pleases most."

Her face lost its cool London fog. In its place came three fingers of red, slowly invading her cheeks. "Is that really how you got into Sanskrit?" Helena said, her voice soft, not brittle. The girl's in love with me already, I thought.

"Really and truly."

"I don't believe a word of it. I'll bet you went into the field because of the girls. Sanskrit is a very sexy subject. Surveys have shown that girl grad students are the loneliest and most willing."

"I see you read *Newsweek* too, Helena. But they never interviewed the gals in Sanskrit. A bunch of females who look like fanatical Jesuit priests down to the stray hairs on their chins. The only fire in them is in their devout eyes. Permafrost ices every erogenous zone between nose and toes—how did your daddy get into Greek?"

Helena covered her laughing mouth with her fingers. "He took the ferry from Cyprus."

The non sequitur floored me. I leaned back and laughed. And Helena, watching me, beamed.

"I like the sound of your voice too," Helena allowed.

When the folksinger appeared and began singing peace songs, I stretched my hand to take Helena's but she slipped away in time. I thought I'd try an intellectual approach. Touch a girl's mind and you've touched her body.

"In peacetime," I quoted Herodotus, "children bury their parents. In war, this natural order is reversed and parents bury their children." I discussed the Vietnam War. I talked about the *Iliad*, the *Odyssey*, comparing translations. Helena's eyes glazed. Brazenly, the hussy did not stifle a yawn. Her forthright ennui astonished me. It laid waste to all my plans.

"Please," she said. "It bores me. I'm sorry, but I don't care to hear any of this. . . . You forget I didn't go to college."

I muttered, "I don't believe it" as I tried for her hand again.

"No, I don't want that." Her second refusal sparked my stubbornness. Now it became a challenge, an adventure. An Everest.

I finished my coffee, but didn't know where to go. What to do next? Drinking is a coward's path and I adore the ratiocinative, contemplative method. *That* much I did get out of the Upanishads. A man's character is his fate, says Heraclitus. What now? Each move was another chess ploy toward an unnamed goal.

"Come," I said, "let's go home. Enough." I didn't wait for her to say yes or no. I stood. She did too.

Outside, however, in the brisk fall air, in the clear night whose chill made breathing a delight, on our way to my car parked on a quiet side street, I seized her hand. With amazing strength, a Chinese wrestler's grip, she twisted away. But I insisted, caught fast, I grasped and did not let go. Acting like a character in a folktale who is told by a sorcerer that the only way to overcome the witch's curse is to seize her hand and no matter what she threatens or how bitterly she cries and pleads, not to dare let go or all will be lost, I grasped and pressed and for the life of me did not let go. I held her hand like a vise. The truth was I didn't want to let her go.

Helena struggled, not moving her body but biting her lip, fighting with her arm, looking as if the struggle was not so much directed at me as at herself. And, anyway, the struggle was no longer between us—the struggle was no longer between us. It was going on somewhere in the distance. Remembered weeks later, how laughable it would have seemed, me fighting to hold a girl's hand. But now it was wrestling with an angel, a struggle for moral dominance, if you will.

So, then, we were battling in some far-off zone. Removed to a colosseum. The eternal struggle between mandala and yantra.

Who was going to win? The one hand did not let the other go. Yet Helena didn't say one word, didn't utter the predictable, Let me go. The witch did not execrate, did not plead for mercy. Once she looked me in the eyes, part fire, part pleading, and like the hero of the folktale, I almost succumbed, almost let the better side of my nature, all compassion, all pity, predominate. But remembering that folktale, the truest of arts, how it reflects life, I did not let go. A neat game was going on down there, in our hands. A game totally independent. It was out of my hands, so to speak. And just when I sensed a sudden blaze of resistance, peaked adrenalin, her hand suddenly relaxed in mine. A series of tense quivers ran through those fingers like shudders through a window pane, as if the stored-up electric energy was spent. I was delirious with joy.

"Well," Helena said, "that's it. Now I'm finished. I didn't want it to go this way. I just wanted to talk to you."

I could have said a lot of things, I could have laughed, I could have sworn her eyes filmed as I slowly loosened my grip.

Now she held my hand. We stood beside my car. "Me, I think with my skin," Helena said. I dropped her hand, held her face. A tremor went through her cheeks. The light in her green eyes softened. "A woman is like a stringed instrument. Touch her. Play her. She must vibrate." Her exact words. I wrote them down that night when I got home.

We sat in the car. Helena turned to me. I threw my arms around her and she, with a movement so quick I could not even catch my breath, began to kiss, passionately, like an unleashed tiger tiger burning bright, probing with tongue, fiercely with a hunger I knew when I first saw her would be there, kissing the edges of my lips, cheeks, forehead, throat, and ears as if she'd known me for years. I slipped my left hand around her waist and to my delight she put my right hand on her breast and said,

"Hold me hold me" as though speaking from another world, the colosseum we'd just returned from, and then slipping her hands behind her back and undoing her bra, not stopping the litany, "Hold me hold me hold me," not stopping it until I was holding her luxuriously springy breasts, mythic breasts one never sees or touches.

"Kiss my glabella," she said.

"Sure."

"That's not my glabella, silly, but, mmm, mmm, go ahead. I like that too. The glabella is the spot between my eyebrows."

"Not in America it ain't."

"Come, let's go home," she said.

I sat in the parlor courting the maid. Her fat, fruity daddy with the thrust-forward paunch and ballerina's frothy walk cultivated to belie his two-hundred-twenty-pound girth (a fatness unbecoming a scholar) hovered nearby. I sensed his large presence somewhere on the ground floor, for the slightest movement of his massive frame created a subtle wind. Then he settled down and began cracking nuts. A comment, I knew, on my late stay. By malevolently cracking nutshells, the old mythicist was sending me symbolic signals as to whose nuts he'd really like to crack. I had two strikes against me. I had been gross enough to get a D in one of his courses (he wrote me, "If you get one more such grade you should give serious thought to choosing to discontinue your graduate studies"), and, besides, he suspected me of corrupting his daughter under his newly acquired, slate-shingled Tudor roof.

Professor Roman Ingelberg cracked, stopped, cracked. I timed the rhythm: crick, rest. Crick, stop. A corrupted daughter was not so terrible. One corrupted by a failure was.

At first, Helena pretended not to hear. So did I. Those weren't nuts being viciously cracked behind the plastic folding doors. Those noises were little aberrations in my ears, result of some mysterious disease.

Still, I asked her, "What's that?"

"My father's studying. He's into mysticism . . . or something like that."

"But what's he doing?"

"Cracking nuts."

"Whose?"

Helena hesitated. I expected her to say—since I'd already put my hands on her and that electric roseate glow was brimming on her roan English cheeks—"Not yours, I hope." For who knows what powers of ritualistic transference that old classicist assumed he possessed.

But Helena only smiled benignly, beaming that chartreuse glaze of her eyes into mine. Just then the professor ceased his cracking. The silence became annoying. At least I knew where he was when he cracked those nuts he didn't eat. Where could the old codger be? Standing behind the cheap folding doors ready to spring in like a satyr at the first obscenity I susurrated into his daughter's pink, nubile ears? Or waiting until she was really corrupted and I unrolled the panty hose from her lubricious thighs. Then I heard a light flick off, and noted the line of darkness at the bottom of the folding doors.

Relieved that the old man—well, not *that* old: mid-fifties, I'd say—had gone upstairs, I moved in for the kill. First a sip of wine for mock civility. I held her hand, felt the electric thrum of current moving through her muscles. Waited for her to say, "Daddy's gone to sleep." Since she said nothing, I assumed he had. I stretched out on the sofa next to her, my head nuzzling her breast. Then, my hand under the black English wool sweater, watching with pleasure how the excitement colored her London face, like pulse beats, or a swerving police car lamp.

One dreamt of these things as one walked out of movie-house doors; one dreamt of those few illusion-laden moments before fantasy has evanesced and the dull cloud of reality settles like an old homey skin about you. But then, insisting, and glad I did, I said to myself, dammit, this one is not going to get away from me, and in a blaze of glory I took and pressed her hand.

She melted, said, "A woman is like an instrument, just touch and pluck the strings." Like an old tender lover she stroked my hand, my fingers, lightly, warmly, then threw herself at me. Her lips were an analog to her accent: brisk, sharp-tasting. A foreign, saffron-colored spice.

"Take off the sweater," I whispered. "No," she said, "not with daddy here."

Looking apologetic, she put her hand on her breast, languidly, like a figure in a medieval painting by whose gesture the artist seeks to catch the viewer's attention.

I heard someone stirring. Footsteps.

Suddenly, the juice was turned off. Helena sprang up. I knew her face was stiff, masked, defensive—the battle lines set on lips and cheeks, as they were before I pressed her hands for the first time and (dis)enchanted her in the few strides between café exit and car door. The air in the room, wine-spiced, close, fogged with musk and smell of love, now cooled. The room grew colder, longer. The colors grayed, the light unveiled.

"My father," she said with a sigh of resignation, "wanders around."

Holding Helena's hand lightly, I wondered if it wouldn't be better to take her out to the car. A flicker of cold crossed her eyes. She withdrew her hand. I shivered.

"What's the matter?"

"I'm worried about Walter."

"Walter. Walter. Walter. That's all I hear. *I'm* with you now."

Helena looked at me as though I weren't there. Then, gazing up at the ceiling, said, "If it weren't for Walter, you wouldn't be here."

"What's with Walter?" I said softly.

"It's a remark I heard my father say on the phone, probably to some member of the promotions committee. He said 'Keinsaltz'—he always calls him that, it means no salt, because he says his limited scholarship is too bland—'has to get on his balls'—daddy never did master American idiom—'and publish more, or else he's going to be an assistant professor 'til the day he dies. His bibliography could be etched on a dwarf's thimble. I don't believe in publish or perish, I believe in publish or languish,' is what daddy said. Poor Walter. Maybe I'll have to marry him."

"Marry him? He's married already. He's old enough to be your father."

"So is my father. Two of my four boyfriends are married. . . . I love married men."

"How come Walter fixed me up with you if he's so stuck on you?"

"He likes to share. So do I. If you had what I have, wouldn't you share?"

I didn't answer.

"Any questions?"

"Which way's the john?"

She told me.

The living room was a long narrow rectangle. One table lamp was lit in the far corner of the room. A muted standing lamp shone dimly on the ink blue sofa by the draped window. Its 40- or 60-watt bulb aimed up at a flaky graying ceiling created an atmosphere that kept people apart. Here Helena, or what was seen of her, slouched. Only her pale face and throat were visible. Even the two English blotches on her face were gone. The rest of her, black sweater and skirt, blended into the sofa. I stepped out behind the plastic folding door into the hall. The nut cracking began again. I followed the sounds. As I came into the no-light of the hallway I saw an apparition.

I saw the apparition in two stages. First a monk dressed in a coarse brown cloak, cowl over shoulders, flitted by, blocking out a dim light. Next I saw him sitting behind a hanging lamp in a wood-lined alcove, cowl over head, fixing his gaze at a row of opened walnuts lined up on index cards. Rooted in place, curious, awed, I was about to step back and tell Helena what I'd seen. Then the monk looked up and I saw that it was her daddy.

"Excuse me, professor, I hope . . ."

"Who are you?" Ingelberg took out his note pad, ready to take my name again as though I were some social equal who would be invited to a party or to deliver a paper (the *Times*, probably).

"Keller," I told him.

"That's right," he said, as if testing me and satisfied I'd come up with the right answer. And if I'd said, "Heller," as I wanted to, would he have said, "That's wrong"?

Ingelberg riffled a page of two and found my name. He pointed to it—"See?"—as if confirming my existence. "We met at Walter's party. Keller, he was quite a student. Not too much ambition, though."

"On the contrary . . . am I disturbing you?"

"Of course not," he chuckled, not at all discomfited by my seeing him in that odd masquerade. "A wise man, I believe it was Thomas Mann—you heard of Thomas Mann, I suppose—said that an esthetic world view is incapable of solving world problems that cry for solution. Nevertheless, esthetics is crucial.

Without esthetics we would be dogs barking at the moon. That's why I don this unseemly garb. To put myself in the medieval mood. I am doing research."

"So I heard." I didn't see what esthetics had to do with nuts, but I suppose that scholars convince themselves that no matter what they do, they contribute to the betterment of the world.

"I am not unaware," Ingelberg said, "of your ironical tone. Indeed, I admit myself—I am going nutty."

"What sort of research is this?"

"Quite complicated. Kabbalistic in essence. I'm probing a verse from the Song of Songs: 'I have gone down into the nut garden.' The Song of Songs is a very erotic piece of work, don't you agree? And this verse has all sorts of sexual, kabbalistic, and mystical implications. Of course, I'm also comparing it to the Arabic and Septuagint translations to catch any nuances. See these walnuts? The dimensions here, the shell, the discarded elements, the hard outer shell, the membrane, the soft meat that represents the delicious within, the penetration into the hidden garden. Hello! Are you with me?" He rapped his knuckles on the desk, calling class—me—to attention and order.

I drooled. Had to contain, slurp back a yawp, a yelp of joy.

"I'm sorry. My mind was wandering. The Song of Songs. Sexual. Mystical."

"Interestingly enough, in medieval kabbalistic Hebrew, the same word—*klipah*—is used for nut shell, the husk, and the rejected negative husk in man's character. And, curiously, *klipah* also means a wicked woman, a Lilith, a Jezebel, who is always present, surrounding the sweet kernel, the soft nutmeat."

"What is it you're trying to do?"

"To see what the phrase really means, what the writer had in mind. If all walnuts are built the same, then . . ."

"Are they?"

"I don't know yet."

"All women aren't built the same."

"True. But they're not nuts." Ingelberg cracked another walnut, opened it. "Perhaps there is a hidden meaning here. I work alone. No colleagues share my passion for nuts."

"Not even Professor Kleinsaltz? His ardor for pecans is unmatched."

"*Kein saltz*," he muttered. "Utterly saltless. Bland."

"Can't his research expertise be useful to you?"

"Keinsaltz is a dear. I love him like a nephew. And," his voice rose, "I resent students bitebacking their teachers with ironic remarks like 'research expertise,' even though he is a proven journal-killer."

"I was not being ironical. And, anyway, as the Greek proverb has it: the truth does not backbite. Or in Sanskrit: fact has no evil tongue."

"You would have a great future in Sanskrit. It is a pity you're not Jewish."

"But I am, sir."

"Well, then, it is a pity you are. Jews cannot possibly hold a Sanskrit chair."

"But you do."

"I don't. And it's not a chair. It is a three-legged stool, firmly buttressed by Greek and Arabic. So, you see, you can't possibly succeed in Sanskrit. Unless, of course, you marry my daughter."

"I'll join the queue."

"What do you mean?"

"There's several married men ahead of me. And I certainly won't jump in ahead of Walter Kleinsaltz."

Ingelberg chuckled. "Helena *is* popular. Everyone wants to marry her. Married men, divorced men, separated men."

"How about single men?"

"Fat chance. I guess there *is* no future for you in Sanskrit."

"Where's the bathroom, please?"

Ingelberg threw back the cowl. "Down the hall. First door on your right. Watch the shells on the sink, please, and lift the seat."

"Poor daddy," Helena said when I came back. She had just finished sealing an envelope. "I'm afraid he's going absolutely nutty. Scholarship and all that sort of stuff has its place, I suppose, but when he got himself that monk's outfit, I realized he was hopeless . . . would you like to listen to some music?"

I wasn't in the mood for music.

"I think I'm going to be celibate for a while," she said, straightening her sweater and swooping her hands down her skirt with a motion of prim finality. "*That* should be fun too. . . . Come, don't you want to hear some records?" she said sweetly. "I've got some lovely Mozarts."

I seized her hands. "Come back into the car with me . . ."

Helena stared straight ahead.

"Well, say something."

I tapped my fingers against my legs.

"How about next Saturday night?" I asked against my will.

"Call me. If my boyfriend hasn't returned by then, we'll see." She jumped up, went to a table drawer. "Here, let me show you his picture."

I banged on the lucite wall between us, not to draw attention, but to wake myself up.

"Not interested," I said.

As I left, she handed me the envelope. She made me promise not to open it until I got home. Of course, as soon as I rounded the corner, I stopped under a street lamp and read:

"If you're going to see Janie—and you should—it wouldn't

be fair to me for you to be seeing her too, especially since I'm almost engaged, and Walter likes me. What's more, your sarcasm and psychological manipulation of Janie shows me what you're liable to do to me, so although I like your body, your psyche frightens me."

I didn't read any more of that rambling neurotic drivel. I had several choices. I could run back to the house, pound on the door. "You're dead wrong. Janie means nothing to me. And what's this all of a sudden about engaged? And Walter? That's a big joke. Here, here's my body. I'm yours. My psyche I left in the glove compartment. It's a very small, harmless psyche, foldable like a map."

And to Walter Kleinsaltz, waking him up in the middle of a dream wherein he's doing research, his wife cooks well and wears sexy contact lenses. "What'd you do to me? You sicked me on to her while running after her yourself? Where's your morals, rabbi? And who is she engaged to? Don't tell me it's you!"

And to Ingelberg: "Professor, I hate to interrupt your research, but you have a very sick, promiscuous daughter. She's getting out of hand, dangling three guys at the same time, one of whom is your saltless Walter. Is that how your yantra rubs off on your own kin?"

I drove off. The lamplight scudded over me like a shadow. It slid on the hood and bumped softly on the roof. All in vain. The emptiness of a Thucydidean battlefield at dusk. Along the dark route home an occasional headlight starkly lit up the roadside bushes. I looked at myself in the rear view mirror. Ingelberg's *klipah*, both husk and Lilith; Janie's *nekomeh*, her wish come true. And a sharp, aching, nut-cracking pain in my loins.

GOLDEN NECKLACE

I didn't know what to expect when I phoned the Principessa from my hotel in Florence.

It began this way. Seven years back, I had seen a travel article in the *New York Times* about three private museums in Tuscany. One in particular engaged me; a noble Florentine family's collection of Renaissance art from the fifteenth and sixteenth centuries, housed in a glorious palazzo. The article stated that the Principessa herself would show this collection on Thursday mornings, for a token fee, but only if persuaded that the viewer was truly an art aficionado and not just a curiosity seeker. I imagined a lengthy interview but figured I could pass.

Now that I was in Italy—I had just attended a meeting of the International Society of Architects in Rome, where I participated in a symposium on synagogue architecture—I was ready to pursue the palazzo. But something happened at the convention that put a patina of melancholy on the rest of my stay. It was one of those chance encounters that most people are more likely to believe when it occurs in fiction than in real life.

We're in the Grand Hall of the Universita di Roma. I had just finished my introductory remarks for the second speaker, Professor Umberto Mignani of Milan. Mignani was giving his slide lecture on the little gem of a synagogue in Casciano, a small town west of Florence. After hundreds of years of continuous residence, the Jewish community had dwindled now to three lonely, elderly souls, Holocaust survivors who refused to leave their birthplace. The synagogue had fallen into desuetude. We were trying to interest the Italian Ministry of Monuments and some private donors to help fund a restoration.

Mignani was ten minutes into his presentation in the darkened hall, focusing on the gorgeous hand-carved Holy Ark, when the silhouette of a latecomer was projected on the screen, followed a moment later by her friend. In the dark I couldn't see either of them. The second woman, perhaps to give her friend time to sit, stood in semi-profile for a heartbeat. At that split instant the light of the 500-watt projector bulb shone on her gold chain and burned its amber glint onto my retina. Something within me bounded, a great leap of my heart. But so potent are the forces of civility and restraint, we keep silent when we should cry out. The chain was in the light for barely a second, but it might as well have been there an hour. My God, my thoughts screamed, that's the chain, and chills waved over me as if a sudden fever had overtaken me.

Now a little golden necklace is not something that one readily remembers, but if it has a second parallel chain from which every half inch or so hang golden oval hoops and from these ovals a vertical needle-wide pendant dangles with a tiny ruby at its tip, then it is a chain one doesn't soon forget. Especially if it's your mother's, and especially if she's wearing it in the only picture you possess of your parents, a three-by-four-inch black-and-white snapshot sent from Amsterdam to a cousin in New York before the war.

I often wondered what my mother looked like when she didn't look like her picture. For that was the only image I had of her. My father I could imagine with different faces, but not my mother. Sometimes I wished there were a way to animate a photo. Insert a snapshot, push a button, and on the screen my mother smiles, throws her head back, and laughs; now she draws closer to kiss me. If I think deeply enough, I can hear her voice, even though my machine hasn't yet perfected sound. Do I want so much to remember my mother that I create memories of her? Or is the only photo that I possess a seed from which grow a hundred moving images of her? In all of them she wears the golden necklace, whose loops move away as if with a life of their own.

That golden chain became a talisman for me. I always carried my mother's photo in my wallet (a copy of course; the original I kept at home). Wherever I traveled in Europe, I went into jewelry shops and asked if they had ever seen a necklace like the one on the picture. Never had I even had the frustrating pleasure of hearing—"Yes, we sold one like that just a few weeks ago." The answer was always no. But at least I had a picture of my parents. Most survivors do not even have that for consideration.

On the dais with six other people, I hope that Mignani will rush through his talk, after which there will be a short break. And then I'd go down into the audience and find the woman with the chain. I hoped I wouldn't sound obsessed or out of control like some madman, anxious to repossess what he presumed was his. I had to remember that although the Germans had stolen the necklace from my mother, the time for repossession by theft was long over. If this were a Hollywood film, I would rush to call the police while Mignani was speaking, have one set of doors locked, station a policeman at the other end, and wait for the woman with the gold chain to approach the door, at which point she would be taken for questioning. But, alas, we live in the real world, as Pascal observed, although there are some who would spell "real" differently.

As Professor Mignani concluded his talk, and the lights went on, I rose quickly and walked to the side of the stage where steps led down to the auditorium. Mignani thinks I'm about to congratulate him, so he anticipates my outstretched hand and sticks his into mine. Which meant I had to praise his presentation. Meanwhile I'm looking over his shoulder to the third or fourth row, just in front of the slide projector, trying to search out the women. But I see only backs. Everyone is heading for the rear doors. Saying, "Excuse me, excuse me, I must get down," I'm about to leap off the stage, when the conference chairman grabs my arm and informs me that since one of the lecturers has to catch a plane the third and fourth speakers would change places. "And by the way," he whispers. "You don't have to go out to the lobby. There's a bathroom backstage." "I have to go," I hissed. "That's why I'm telling you," he said. "Go here. Don't fight the crowd."

That's how it is. When you're in a rush, even double entendres get in the way.

I elbowed my way politely through the crowd. But the two women had slipped away from me.

I waited in the aisle for the audience to return. The chain, illuminated by that powerful projector bulb, was printed on my mind as though upon photographic paper. I waited to catch sight of the two women. I scanned faces, watched groups of twos. How did she get that chain? I wondered. More than fifty years had passed. Who sold it to whom? Had it been torn from my mother's neck? Or had she given it up placidly, too afraid to resist? Perhaps my father, fearing for her life, had told her to give it up when the Germans barked: Anyone with gold, hand it over. Anyone caught with gold will be shot.

I thought I spotted the two women, but these women sat in the back, unadorned by necklaces. By the time everyone returned, the hall was full again, save for the two seats in the third row. I ran out to the lobby. Empty too.

Agitated and distressed, frustrated, depressed—there weren't sufficient words in the English language to describe the gnawing emptiness in my soul—I rushed back to the stage. I asked the conference chairman if he knew those two latecomers. He had no idea but suggested I call the conference office. The secretary didn't know either. There were no ticketed seats, hence no list of attendees. I was at the end of the trail.

But how long can one mourn the loss of a thing one never possessed? It was the reverse of the old Yiddish proverb that my father loved to quote: When is a poor man happy? When he finds what he has lost. I had lost what I never found. I shook off my frustration and turned my attention to the Principessa's private museum. Forward is my motto.

Still, I must add that after the conference I walked around the streets of Rome, imagining I would run into that woman. And suppose I find her, what would I do? Plead? Cajole? Scream? Explain? No, I would lure her into a dark alley, seize her, bind her eyes with a handkerchief, remove my gold chain, and flee. But wouldn't I be interested in how it got to her? History, provenance, and all that? How easy it is! Crimes committed in the imagination remove security guards, police, witnesses, alarms, and other people from the scene. In mind crimes, the victim even lifts up her chin, puts her hand behind her neck, undoes the little latch, and presents you with the object you want. She even directs you to the closest Metro stop or points out the best street for hailing a cab. In mind crimes you are always absolved of culpability. In any case, a man can't be convicted for retrieving what's been stolen from him. Even the Talmud, I am told, states that he who steals from a thief is absolved of guilt.

I take out the photo. In the European manner, my parents do not smile when a picture is taken. I want to remember my mother smiling. I see her bending over me when she brings me to the Dutch farmer who hid me, the farmer who saved me. I imagine she smiled at me, how could she not? Even though I was only two, I remember the light of that smile. Some lights never dim no matter how much darkness envelops them. Even a black hole could not swallow up the light of her smile. She hugs and kisses me, and as she bends over the little loops of her golden necklace move forward and hang straight down. My father places the palms of his hands on my head. Only later did I realize that he had blessed me, blessed me with life and peace, as fathers do their children on Friday nights when they return from the synagogue. I wish I could have done the same for them. My mother's face is over me as she smiles goodbye but doesn't say it's a last goodbye. But perhaps she feels in her heart it's a last goodbye, for two tears roll down her cheeks. I know now how desperately she wanted to believe it was not goodbye but only *au revoir*. And as she bends over me the ovals of her golden necklace touch my chin. That was the last thing of my mother's that touched me.

After the conference I took the train to Florence. It was a sunny June morning. The Tuscan hills and fields, visible from Piazzale Michelangelo, were not far away. There is a special fragrance in the early morning Italian air, soft, tangy, slightly damp—perhaps from the daily scrubbings the sidewalks get every morning—but it doesn't last long. If one is lucky, one can also get the tantalizing and evanescent whiff of jasmine before the roar of traffic shatters the fragile post-dawn silence and brings particulate fumes and noises to pollute the Florentine air.

Back home I would have waited 'til 9 a.m. to call. But since life starts early in Italy, by eight-thirty I was in a little phone booth in the lobby of my hotel, dialing the number listed in the *New York Times* article. The phone rang and rang. No one answered. Perhaps after seven years, I thought, the number on the brittle, yellowing newsprint was no longer valid. Maybe the Principessa had been flooded with so many curiosity seekers that she stopped the tours. Maybe she changed her number. Maybe she moved. (Fat chance, as I later discovered. Countries would sooner change flags, modes of government, than princesses move from their ancestral palazzos. Continents drift; princesses stay put.) Still, I was hopeful. I called the Florence Tourism Bureau. The girl on duty heard my story, knew about the Principessa, and told me that she now had a new number.

As I dialed, I wondered how I could prove that I wasn't a dilettante. No one loves museums more than I, I fancied telling her. (She probably excelled in English, and my saying "me" would mark me a boor.) Works of art hang on my walls; nay, on the screen of my memory. That phrase, if she understood English—how could she not, having just admired my sophisticated grammar?—should strike at her heart like a Tintoretto. Or was it Pintoretto? I can't pass a gallery without going in, I continue my litany. All the museum doormen know me. The stacks of auction house catalogs in my apartment are so high I use some as a base for my glass table that bends at the corners like Dali's drooping watches due to the weight of my many massive art tomes.

But it was all a lie.

As an architect, I really wanted to see not her paintings but her palazzo, which the *Times* had called glorious. In my view, buildings were art, and artworks just fleeting décor. Truth was, museums—except for their structure and shape (the Gug in

NYC, the Louvre and the Pompideau in Paris)—bored me. It annoyed me that painting was the only art form so closely tied to commercial interests. Years ago, poor Van Gogh, freezing in his icy garret, had to cut off one ear and trade it for a pair of earmuffs. Recently, one of his paintings sold for fifty million dollars, enough to buy all of Holland and a lifetime supply of earmuffs for all Dutchmen. The entire art world was one huge stock market. Not only was art bought and sold like peas and pears, but artists too were traded like ball players. The League of Artists was the third major league. A picture of a picture in an art book moved me more than the real thing, especially if it had buildings in it, like a Canaletto. And the colors were usually better. My favorite day in New York was Monday, when the galleries and museums were closed. But palazzos, and the unique people who resided in them, fascinated me. That's why I wanted to see the Principessa's collection. In short, like a good reader, I judged a book by its cover.

"*Pronto*," said a woman at the other end of the line.

"*Parla inglese?*" I asked.

"Yes, I do," she said in unaccented English.

"Is this the Principessa?"

"No."

"May I speak to her?"

"She left yesterday for Chicago."

I looked up at the mahogany walls of the tight little phone booth. I unbuttoned my jacket, slipped out of it. Tomorrow was the only Thursday of my four-day stay in Florence. My "Oh" did not hide my disappointment.

Her commiserating "You sound so sad" surprised me.

"Well, I read that she shows her collection only on Thursdays."

"True, but she's coming back on Sunday."

"The very day I'm leaving."

"Are you a collector?" she asked.

"Well, yes," preparing myself for the test like a character in a medieval Italian fairy tale. Perhaps this woman, the Principessa's assistant, was authorized to administer the test and then show the collection. But at that moment all the reasons I'd rehearsed to prove myself bona fide evaporated. I felt hot in this cramped phone booth. I wiped the perspiration from my face and opened the door a notch. Cool air flowed in.

"You see, for years I've been saving a beautiful *New York Times* piece about the Principessa's small private museum."

"You have?" she said delightedly. "She loved that piece. You must be very determined."

"I am. Are you related to her? Sister? Cousin? Daughter?"

"Oh no. I'm just a friend of the family."

"You speak English beautifully."

"Thank you." She laughed. "I'm an American, Sarah Waterman from Minneapolis, and I've known the family for years. Now I'm sort of a long-term house guest. . . . All right. Look. Would you like to come over tomorrow morning and I'll show you around here?"

"Why sure. Thanks."

"But I still don't know your name."

"Joseph," I said. "Joseph Ginsburgh."

The palazzo, rimmed by a high iron fence, stood on a quiet street. It was a rather cool morning. The sun was hidden by an overcast sky. I walked through the open gate into a small cobblestoned courtyard about twenty-five feet long that led to a rather unimaginative and plain three-story gray stone building. I had seen palazzos here and in Sienna, in Venice and Urbino. This one wasn't glorious at all. I wondered what the *Times* writer had seen in it.

I stood under the open high arch. Judging by several holes in the thick stone doorposts and the two-inch holes bored into the right and left sides of the lintel, huge oaken doors had once hung there. One can still see these ten- or twelve-foot doors in many old apartment buildings, into which normal-size doors have been cut. Years ago, this high arch permitted a horse-drawn carriage with a driver seated on top to clear the entranceway. At the turn of the century, carriages unloaded passengers and goods here. Now it was an open-air, high-ceilinged antechamber. The carriages long gone, now a Maserati and a Jeep were parked on the far side, almost out of view. A curving stone stairway to the left led up to the main quarters. On the right, near the arch where I stood, seen behind a little window, was a receptionist's tiny cubicle. An old retainer—I don't know what other name to give him—came out to greet me.

"*Buon giorno*, Signora Waterman," I said.

"*Momento*," he replied. He opened the door of a small wooden wall box, lifted the receiver of an old black telephone, cranked the handle three times, and said a few words.

Just then, a woman in red, in her late thirties or early forties, short, pretty, petite, with small, finely chiseled features and a little aquiline nose, breezed by with a determined, in-control stride, holding a shopping bag. A thought flashed—a *yidishe ponim*, a Jewish face—then faded. She greeted the old man familiarly, patted his cheek, looked at me—did she approve of my jacket? disapprove of my tieless shirt?—and said, "Hi. I'll be right down. Why don't you take a peek into our garden?"

I took a few steps to the second arch, spanned by a spoked gate. The gate was locked. I looked into the garden, scanned the sculptures, the rose bushes, the flowering shrubs, scores of citrus trees. A fifteen-foot-high stone wall ran on both sides of the broad garden for what seemed like three city blocks.

A tap on the shoulder made me turn.

"Hi. I'm Sarah," and she gave me her warm hand.

She wore a red cable-knit sweater over a white blouse, the little white collar of which was tucked over the sweater, and tight blue slacks.

I thanked her for inviting me.

"Actually, it's not my invitation, it's the Principessa's. You see, I figured I'd do what she would have done. She certainly would have invited you, so that's what I did." Said with a little girl's self-congratulatory brightness.

The old man emerged from his little cubicle with a note, which she looked at and slipped into her pocket. The man was older than the seventy-five I had thought him to be. Short, white-haired, obsequious, he was probably in his eighties. I imagined him having served the family since boyhood.

"Tonio's a dear," Sarah said, putting her arm around his shoulders. The man smiled shyly.

"Old family retainer?"

"Precisely. His father worked here all his life too, and so did his grandfather."

Now she let go of Tonio and he returned to his cubicle.

"Come, let me show you the garden," she said.

Sarah removed a large key from her pocket and opened the gate. Although we were in the heart of the city, and long streets ran on each side of the stone walls, here in the garden it was still. The trees, bushes, and statuary all seemed to absorb the incessant din of traffic.

The garden was impressive, yes, but it was the palazzo I wanted to see.

As if reading my mind, she suddenly asked, "So what is it you actually wanted to see?"

"What I mentioned yesterday. The museum."

The weather on her face, spring-like, buds blossoming, suddenly changed. Her cheeks, her lips tightened, as if crimped by the words she was about to say:

"Oh, I'm so sorry. That I can't show you. Only the Principessa has the keys."

"But I thought that's why you invited me . . . that you were going to show it to me."

"No, no, no. You must have misunderstood. I'm not permitted, not authorized. Only she has the keys. Anyway, the collection isn't here. It's in their other palazzo, the beautiful one on the other side of the river."

"Oh . . . so that's . . ."

"I thought you'd also be interested in the grounds here." Sarah plucked an orange. "Here. Take one. They're quite delicious."

I admired the way she moved so seamlessly, cleverly too, from frankness to sweet talk. I can't say I liked it, but I admired it. I often wondered whether the border between ingenuous and ingenious wasn't purposely fuzzy, linguistically. The old gents who founded the language were right on the mark.

I began peeling the orange, looked for a wastebasket. But this wasn't a public park. Sarah held out her hand, palm up, almost like a beggar, asking me to drop the peels into her hand. Playing along, I dropped a couple of pieces into her outstretched palm. She promptly threw them into the bushes.

"I could have done that myself," I said pleasantly. "I didn't need an intermediary." Sarah smiled. Her eyes flashed.

Was there an electricity in the air as the two of us stood there?

Perhaps she would invite me upstairs to see the living quarters. I imagined a dining room with a glass-smooth thirty-foot-long mahogany table. She'd sit me down, ring a little silver bell, and a wine steward would emerge with a bottle of Romanee-Conti 1985 Bordeaux ($3,000 a bottle) or a Mouton Rothschild 1929 Bordeaux ($9,000) from their private wine cellar, and a servant would enter with a silver tray on which stood two hand blown Venetian goblets with a faint rose blush visible when held up to the light, and then another servant would bring out a purple cushion on which rested my mother's gold necklace, after which she'd invite me for a stroll through the garden into a private bower.

"Does the Principessa live here all by herself?"

"With her husband."

"And when they dine . . . I sort of imagine an enormously long mahogany dining room table, she at one end, and he at the other."

"Actually," she said, walking with me along the path, "she sits in the middle, as befits royalty. Did you know she's the highest-ranking royalty in Italy today?"

"I thought that royal rank no longer exists in this democratic republic."

"It doesn't. But only on the outside. Here, on the inside, within their circles, it's very much alive, and they're always conscious of it in each other's presence. For instance, when Prince Charles was here recently, since he outranks her, he sat in the middle and Sofia to his right."

"Wealthy, huh?" I said casually.

"Enormously. They themselves don't know how much money they have. It's all in land, olive groves all over Italy, and vineyards too, miles and miles of property."

"Then why do they open up their museum? Do they need the money from those Thursday morning tours?"

Sarah laughed. "*That's* not the money they're interested in. You see, by opening up their collection once a week to the public, their palazzo is considered a museum and they pay no taxes on that vast and valuable property."

I looked at Sarah. A pretty young woman. Maybe there was something between her and the Prince. She hadn't said that the husband had gone to Chicago. Or perhaps between her and the Principessa.

"And how do you fit in?"

She laughed again. "Me? I'm just a beloved house guest who tags along. Actually, I befriended their daughter in college. They take me everywhere, all the festivals in Europe, the film festivals in Cannes and Venice, to Bath and Bournemouth, to Davos. They mingle with princes and premiers and world-class artists like Zubin and Pav, Pinkie and Yo. . . . But enough of us. Let's hear about you. What do you do, Joseph?"

I was surprised she remembered my name.

There were so many things I could have told her—as long as it wasn't the truth. For despite the fact that this was liberal Italy, with its basically beneficent attitude toward Jews, who knew what was the attitude of this house, this family? Anyway, surely these nobles wouldn't be interested in synagogue architecture. So I let my imagination run wild. What do I do? I could have said, You know those T-shirts with photos on them? Well, I invented a process whereby the photo of the person wearing a plain white T-shirt comes out on the front just through bodily contact. It's a photobionic process I invented. Wow, she says, can you show me how it works? Gladly, but I don't have any samples with me. My baggage was lost, sent to Melbourne by mistake.

I could have said I was a reader.

A reader, she'd say. I heard of writers, but a reader? Is that a profession?

People read for a living, I'd say. Did you ever hear of editors?

Is that what you do? You're an editor?

No, a reader.

For a living? Well, yes. Read in order to live, Flaubert observed. Or to put it in an earlier age, remember the Bible—but who reads the Bible nowadays? I chuckle—Ezekiel's vision? In it the prophet is ordered to open his mouth and read a book by eating it. In other words, to understand its meaning by ingesting it. *Id est* (with no Yiddish pun—Jew, eat!—intended): reading in order to live.

I decided to go with that.

"I'm a reader," I said aloud.

"I stopped reading after college," she said.

"You know what Flaubert said?"

"No."

"He said: Read in order to live. . . . Reading is conversing with the absent, said Augustine."

"Socrates argued against reading," was Sarah's riposte. "He said books are useless tools, since they can't explain what they say but repeat the same words over and over again. But on rare occasions, I'll take a book to bed in order to fall asleep."

"In his *Rules of Christian Civility*, St. Jean-Baptiste de La Salle thunders out against idle people who read in bed."

Sarah gave an ambiguous smile. "You seem to have an answer for everything. As though our conversation were preordained and you've rehearsed your answers. Still, Chaucer's Duchess liked to read in bed. Remember . . . 'The other night, when I might not slepe, upon my bedde I sat upright and took me a booke. . . .'"

"How do you know that?"

"I majored in English," she said, which made me smile. "But I stopped reading soon after . . . maybe because of that major. And anyway, I'm not that familiar with Christian civility. It's out of my league." She paused. "Is listening to music idleness too?"

"I'm not the one to judge." Then I stopped smiling. "Sorry, I was joking about being a reader."

"So what do you really do?" Sarah asked amicably, with a little flirtatious tilt of her head.

And in the spirit of the palazzo, with its removal from the space and time of modernity, its isolation from noisy, motorcycle-polluted Florence, with this palazzo that seemed to float, removed, on a sixteenth-century cloud, as if we were frozen on a painting, unencumbered by the reality of matter beyond the frame, in the spirit of all this, I heard myself saying that I'm a composer, that I was on a one-year fellowship at the Academy of Rome, that I specialize in string quartets that don't shriek or cry out against melody by grating the ears, that even as a youngster I composed, solely in my head, works that had already been written by Haydn and Beethoven—I did his late quartets first, then graduated to the early ones—but I didn't know it until I heard them years later.

"How truly amazing!" she said.

"I know," I said. "I can't get over it myself."

"Did you ever write them down?"

"No. When I composed them, I knew nothing about notation. I hear the melody in my mind, on an oboe, tuned to A of course."

"Can you sing one of your melodies?"

"Is there a piano upstairs? I could play one for you."

"They only have a harp. But I'd love to hear one of your melodies. Why don't you sing it?"

I thought for a moment, stalling for time, then sang one of the standard Sabbath table hymns.

"It sounds familiar."

"My tunes get around. Maybe you heard the Castelnuovo-Tedesco arrangement." Just then a soft thud. A lemon had fallen.

"In the olden days," Sarah said, "a tenor would crack a wine goblet."

"Indoors," I said, "I crack glass. Outdoors, fruit falls. Grapes, usually. Pomegranates, when I'm in minor key."

Sarah smiled again. I could tell she enjoyed my sense of the absurd.

There was a pause. The absolute silence in music that Haydn adored.

No sounds of traffic. Stood still Firenze.

I wanted to change the subject. "And you, a little girl, born and bred in Minneapolis, Minnesota, hobnob with counts and princes!"

Sarah plucked a lemon, weighed it in her hand. Would she offer it to me? She hefted it two or three more times, then placed it near the base of the tree, next to the fallen fruit.

Sarah looked me straight in the eye. "You said your name was Ginsberg."

"Not Ginsberg, boorg. I spell it urgh. Like Gettysburgh."

She made a face. "No matter how you spell it, Ginsberg is still Ginsberg. Those who drop the h from Cohen are still Cohen."

What was she driving at? I remembered how I felt in the phone booth the other morning, closed in a coffin-like space, wanting air. Was Sarah taking on the snootiness of royalty? Did she mean something other than what she was saying?

"What are you trying to say?" I asked. That I'm hiding my identity behind an urgh?

"Not important," she said. A gloom came over me, just as it had in Rome when the golden necklace slipped away from me.

"I wasn't born in Minnesota. I was born in Germany."

The air changed. Again a change of season. The lemons on the ground sprayed their bitterness. No wonder the Cohen lecture. So she's a German. I wondered who her parents might have been. Who was her father? Was it he who pulled my parents out of the train? Italy and Germany. The Axis redux.

I had sensed, when I set foot here, that this place was the essence of gentileness, but I didn't realize how much.

"Germany," I hissed, getting back at her. "Germany," I repeated, as if it were an execration, as if I'd bitten into the lemon she had discarded. "The Italians, I found, don't much like Germany or the Germans."

I felt suddenly hot, as if a heat wave had compressed itself and dropped its cape over me. The morning coolness was gone. I took off my jacket and placed it on a statue. Mimicking me ("You're right," Sarah said, "it is hot."), she crisscrossed her hands and pulled her sweater over her head. I was so busy watching this intimate gesture, the red cloth rising like a little flag, the form of her slim body, that I didn't at once notice what was around her neck. Like Hermann Hesse said in one of his stories, You look all over the world for something and then discover it in your own back yard.

When I finally saw what my eyes were looking at, I leaped forward and seized her arms.

"Where did you get that?"

"Get what? Stop it! You're hurting me."

"The chain," I hissed. "That necklace!"

"Help!" she screamed. "Tonio! Tonio!"

"That's my necklace," I shouted.

"Help!" she shouted, struggling. "What? What do you mean your chain? What are you talking about?"

But in this faraway bower, old Tonio could not hear.

"Your German father gave it to you, right? The one who took . . ."

But as soon as I said "German" she burst into tears. And I mean that word "burst." It wasn't an incremental sadness that ends in tears. Her weeping came at once. Instantly. Instantly, there was full-fledged wailing, keening, mourning that tore at my heart. Then, as if paralysis had overtaken her, a moment later, she stood open-mouthed, mute, like in a silent movie. She rubbed her left forearm, breathing quickly, as if gathering strength. Then the words tore out of her, hot steam hissing through a tiny opening.

"I wasn't born in Germany Germany, you idiot! I was born in a DP camp. My parents were survivors, but the Germans murdered my two brothers, brothers I never met. My name is Sarah Wasserman, which was changed to Waterman."

The long mahogany dining room table swirled. It spun around in a room too narrow for it to spin. Sitting on the table, I watched the carousel of lemon trees bobbing up and down around me, like toy horses with their riders. But there was no music. I wished I were one of the statues. I wished I were dead.

"Forgive me!" I shook my head to clear the jumbling thoughts. For a moment I thought of falling to my knees in contrition. I spread my arms in a pleading stance. "I'm sorry. I'm so sorry."

I wanted to embrace her, hug her, console her, press her to me.

"My God, I thought you were going to kill me."

"I'm sorry. Please forgive me."

"What got into you? And what's this about the necklace?"

I looked down. "It's my mother's," I whispered.

"Impossible. The Principessa gave it to me. It must be an heirloom. And, anyway, how do you know it's your mother's? It could be a coincidence of design. Are you a goldsmith too, like Botticelli, in addition to being a reader and a composer? I dare say, Mr. Ginsboorg," she mocked my pronunciation, "you're an all-around Renaissance man. And such strong forearms too."

I let her sarcasm fly by me.

"My parents did not survive," I said. "They were Dutch Jews and were probably on the same train as Anne Frank."

"Oh my God. And you?"

"They brought me in time to a Dutch farmer who hid me."

Now I took the picture from my wallet. One image is worth hundreds of caustic barbs. "Here. Take a look."

Sarah held the photo. "Oh my God," she said. "It's . . ." And she gave the snapshot back to me. Was it tears I saw again in her eyes? Or were my eyes filling over, causing me to see tears everywhere. "And I'm . . . Oh my God . . . and it's on me."

"You also wore it the other day. I saw it on you, lit up by the projector bulb?"

"Where?"

"In Rome, last Monday, around 11 a.m. The symposium on synagogue architecture."

"Were you there?"

"Of course, how else could I have seen you? What were you doing there?"

"The Principessa has an interest in the Casciano synagogue."

"But you came late."

"Our driver had a flat. We had to hail a cab. Ah . . ." She pointed a finger at me. "I thought you looked familiar. That's where I saw you. On the podium. . . . Why didn't you say you were an architect?"

"I don't like to brag," I said, choking on the words.

She tilted her head. "But you weren't shy about your composing skills."

I said nothing.

"Is that why you came here? To fetch the necklace?"

"No." I laughed. "How could I know where you were? I couldn't even make out your face in the dark. *This* is coincidence, although the Indian philosophers deny coincidence, saying that everything is fated, and maybe so. Believe me, I tried to find out who those two women were. I ran down into the audience after you during the break to try to speak to you, but you were gone."

"We had to leave. Why did you want to speak to me?"

"Not to you. To the necklace, lit up by that bright projector bulb as you stood there, forever it seemed." Again the vertiginous swirl of objects, and a sharp pain in the front of my head. I didn't know what I was saying. Speak to a necklace! Did I want to speak to a golden necklace? I wanted to speak to my mother.

What now? I thought. The necklace is hers and it's mine. Defying one of Newton's basic laws. But still, it was possible, for I remembered reading that scientists had successfully demonstrated that an atom could be in two places at the same time.

And then—was I dreaming it, dream-wishing it?—it seemed to me that she put her hands to the back of her neck and a moment later pressed the necklace into my hand.

"No," I said.

"It's yours," she said. "I don't want to ask her how she got it. The Principessa's family saved many Jews. They were hidden in their villages. But German officers were billeted in many of the palazzos here, even against the will of the owners. Who knows who the admirers of Sofia's mother were? Or how they expressed their gratitude?"

"Aren't you going to tell me where the closest Metro stop is?"

"Firenze has no subway. You're thinking of Rome."

"And where's the purple cushion?" bubbled out of me.

"You and the absurd have a thing going, don't you? Do you get that from all your reading? You sound like a bachelor," she continued without a pause. "Only bachelors have time for so much reading."

"Yes. But not confirmed."

Sarah laughed.

"Books light my way. I live in order to read."

"And I just live. Period," she said. "A book can't take the place of the world, Kafka observed."

"So you do read."

"When other options fail."

"A book must be the axe for the frozen sea within us," I said.

"Living melts the ice faster," Sarah said. "For an architect, you seem to be much of a dreamer."

"I build castles in the sky."

I held my mother's chain. "From the dead to the living. I can't believe I'm holding it in my hands. Wait a minute. I'm straying from what I really wanted to say. The Principessa won't miss it?"

"Would she miss one of her olive trees?"

I looked at Sarah. Through her eyes into the past. "If you were born in a DP camp, then this whole royal scene . . ."And I made a gesture with my wrist like a drunkard trying to speak. "If you were born in a DP camp, your parents were probably from Poland, right? Then you must talk Yiddish."

"*Avadeh*," she said. "*Avadeh ken ikh redn Yiddish*. Of course, I speak Yiddish. It's my first language."

"And your parents came to the U.S. in 1947 when America finally opened up its gates."

"No, they went straight to Israel, where they stayed 'til I was ten."

"This is too much." I laughed. "Then you must speak Hebrew too."

Sarah said a couple of sentences in Hebrew. "Actually, Hebrew is my native tongue. Too bad you're not staying 'til Monday. I'd have asked Sofia to open the museum for you on Sunday. The note Tonio just gave me said that Sofia called. She's coming back Saturday night instead of Sunday."

"I'm leaving Sunday morning." I looked at her. She stood calmly, but not quite as still as the statue from which I removed my jacket.

"Sarah, I'm going to make a little speech, but I have no words." I took her hand and kissed it. "Is there anything I can do for you?"

She pressed her index finger to her cheek. "No, not really. But wait, yes, there is."

"What? Anything!" Maybe she'd say, Come up and have lunch with me.

"Spell Gettysburg correctly. It doesn't end with an h."

Then she took my hand, warmly I think. Again there was a merry glint, a flash in her eyes. Maybe, I thought, I'd put off my Sunday morning flight. Perhaps it was fated that I leave on Monday. Maybe Tuesday. That I indeed see the palazzo I'd waited seven years to see. Maybe it was fated, like our preordained conversation. Like the golden necklace that both my mother and she had worn.

It wasn't until I crossed the cobblestoned courtyard and passed through the outer gate that I heard her call to me from under the high archway.

"And the next time anyone asks you what you do—follow Flaubert and Augustine, Plato and the Bible too."

"To wit?" I cried out to her across the cobblestones.

"Tell the truth."

"Okay! I want to live too," I shouted.

And her radiant smile transported me, like the swift bright light of the projector bulb, like the books that light my way, through the gate and into the garden.

SAY IT ISN'T SO, MR. YIDDISH

Jerusalem, it was known all over Jerusalem, the holy city, that Shmulik Gafni, Overlyfull Professor, Chairman and Distinguished University Researcher of Yiddish Language, Literature, Culture, and Folklore on the Mendl and Sadie-Yentl Eizenbahn Chair of Yiddish Studies at the University of Israel, the most famous scholar of Yiddish in the world, not only by his own estimation but in the estimation of others, for instance a fellow scholar, Sh. Meichl-Rukzak, who was himself a leading candidate for that honorific, in an interview with the *New York Times* (with the help of a translator) called Shmulik Gafni "Mister Yiddish" (but everyone, aware of their rivalry, said it was just a sarcastic jibe), married for more than forty years was he, forty not being the mythical forty of the Bible, a ubiquitous Biblical cipher, but a metaphor for a long long stretch of time, which by all objective accounts a forty-year marriage truly is, married not to two or three women, mind you, like most non-Yiddish scholars, with a graduate assistant and/or secretary on the side (the female side, to be sure), for Yiddish scholars tend to be more conservative (one to one-and-a-half wives at most), forty not being an aggregate of marriage years, a sum of various unions, but the number of years he'd been with one woman,

Batsheva was her name, and for her there was only one man too, a good-looking, bright, and witty man was Shmulik, who had attained the Biblical three score and ten (he loved Biblical numbers, and names too, witness his choice of mate) in good health more or less (the less was a minor heart attack some years back, for which he briefly took medications and, reluctantly, after much coaxing by Batsheva, now grumblingly wore an electric monitor called the *Chaver*, or friend, based on the American model known as the "Companion," which he never yet had to use, didn't know the workings of, except maybe press a button), with sparkling gray eyes compressing a gleam that could be ironic, sardonic, impatient, and disarmingly affectionate in rather quick order, a mellifluous baritone speaking voice, which even when he spoke privately at home rang out with a lecturer's boom whose authority, charm, and fluidity of nuance excited all his girl students, especially when he smiled and his powerful teeth shone and the laugh lines at the corner of his wolf-gray eyes crinkled and he ran his hand through his full head of wavy steel-gray-sprinkled hair, hair that once years back when he was on a research trip an old Italian barber in New York held up like a bunch of asparagus and said to him, "You gotta healthy heada hair, you never ever gonna getta balda," a prognostication that held true, even forty years later, and a look in his eyes that combined boyish shyness, even at seventy, and worldly assurance, with a thirty-four-year-old son, Yosef, twin daughters, Rivka and Rachel, forty-three, and twin granddaughters, Penina and Zehava (one from each daughter, explanation coming), one of whom, the elder, though both were born precisely at the same second, now had a one-year-old son, which made a great-grandfather of Shmulik Gafni, a name he hadn't had of course back home in Warsaw, his pre-World War II hometown, but which he changed from Weingarten, "wine garden" (easy enough, right? who says you don't know Yiddish?), an imposing name with rhythm and élan, with trisyllabic balance and a triad of different vowel neumes, even a tone-deaf man saying "Weingarten" sounded as though he'd just finished rehearsing for a lieder recital, Shmulik dropping the Weingarten after being told privately, discreetly, but in no uncertain terms that the authorities in Israeli higher education, 1950 was the year, just two years after Independence, not too keen on Yiddish in the first place, in fact, truth to say, because we offer here no make-believe, but the whole truth and nothing but the truth, as American court clerks state with such grandiloquence, the Israel bureaucrats (all born in Eastern Europe and Yiddish speaking) looking down their quintessential Jewish noses at this Diasporic Yiddish language that threatened (so they asseverated) to compete with the ancient Hebrew, even though all the founding fathers of Israel were born into that supple, juicy, evocative, folk-saturated, wise, witty and image-laden Yiddish tongue, and greedily imbibed, yes, sucked it in with their mama's milk, and spoke it more naturally and felicitously than Hebrew, which was strong on verbs but weak on modern nouns and the subtleties of adverbs and adjectives, and how can you run a nation just on verbs anyway?, but run it they did, in fact race and gallop in it, around it and through it with verbs, moxie, faith, and smuggled weapons too, Shmulik was told that these higher ed officials would look more kindly on his efforts to establish Yiddish studies at the University of Israel if he wouldn't have such a blatantly *potch-in-pawnim* (slap-in-the-face, for the handful of you out in the boondocks who haven't yet mastered Yiddish) Diasporic Jewish name but a more acceptable Hebraized one, Gafni, for instance, remember this was two years after Independence when nationalism was so intense it bordered on jingoism, although in Israel they hadn't heard of the word and wouldn't know what it meant even if they heard it, but words are created for situations, movements, and moods and not vice versa, and the mood then in Israel rejected all foreign-sounding (read: Jewish-sounding) names, hiding it under the protective purple cloak of Hebrew, when everyone knew that Weingarten had been around for two hundred years or more and Gafni hadn't even been around the block yet much less around the corner, and anyone who ever met a Gafni would at once say, "You used to be Weingarten, right?" just like if anyone met a phony concoction of a name like Har-paz, he'd smirk and say, "Ah, né Goldberg, hill of gold", but you know that from Bach's famous Variations, but Gafni it was, folks, and Gafni it had to be, Gafni, meaning "my vine"—close enough, but that wasn't what was known all over Jerusalem, it won't be too long before you *do* know what was known, or rather "known," all over Jerusalem, and a juicy bit of knowledge it was—close enough to his paternal family name, but this Gafni business, as far as Shmulik Weingarten was concerned, was merely part of the "i" suffix name syndrome that most Israelis succumbed to and that most Europeans assumed were Italian, surnames like Gafni, Magdani, Zehavi, Caspi, Crispi, and Crunchi, modern stand-ins for all the delicious, age-old, authentic Jewish names that the goyim had imposed upon the Jews and that the Jewish goyim in Israel were imposing on Ashkenazi names. (Question: What was the difference between the goyim there in Europe in the 1700s forcing you to take a name and the Jews here gently twisting your forearm to take a Hebrew-sounding name? Answer: Here you didn't have to pay for it). But there was a price, mind you, a mighty awful price to pay anyway, far costlier than the gold the Jews had to fork over to Christian authorities two hundred-fifty years ago for their new Jewish family names, for now if a family member, let's say a Holocaust survivor or a Russian immigrant, came to Israel and sought you out in the telephone book or on the population list of the Interior Ministry, he would never find you, for fine old Jewish names like Ginsburg, Brandenburg, Silverberg, Goldberg, and Iceberg all became Hebraified, deracinated, a kind of nose job on the paterfamilias moniker, but Shmulik Weingarten reluctantly agreed to gafnify his name if it would help, and indeed it did, for Yiddish studies, due to him and his Polish Jewish obstinacy and his passion for everything Yiddish, and thanks to the Yiddish supporters he mustered all over the land, the University of Israel Global Yiddish Department developed into a world center, perhaps *the* world center for Yiddish, competing with and even superseding the superb one at the Hebrew University, an "address" as he laughingly called it one day many years ago during his own interview with a foreign correspondent for the *New York Times* as he held his little twin daughters (one of whom, grown up now of course, had become a grandmother just a year ago) on his knees, but it was the other twins, a score of so years later, who were called a medical miracle, still being written up by doctors and parapsychologists and of course photographed, for they were two daughters born, one each to Shmulik's twin girls, Rivka and Rachel, at precisely the same time, at 7:16 a.m., which aroused the curiosity of geneticists, who found that the little sweetypies had the same DNA, hence they were twins, even though emanating from two different wombs, the which were presumably inseminated at the same time by two different men, but enough of medicine and magic and the hocus pocus of DNA, which science, important as it is, impertinent wags and wits have dubbed Don't Know Anything, for it is Yiddish and sex—not as unlikely a twinning, or coupling, by your grace, as you might assume—that here interests us, entwines us, betweens us, to coin a wordploy, which by the way is what fiction is all about, wordploy, although what is being said here, what was known all over Jerusalem, and remember, what's known isn't always true and what's true isn't always known, so what was "known" all over Jerusalem is neither fictive speculation nor imaginative rumination, but pure unadulterous truth (truth in the sense that it truly was known but not necessarily true) that Shmulik Gafni was reportedly plucking grapes from a wine garden not truly his own, having been seriously involved, so it was stage-whispered all over Jerusalem, which in fact meant all over Israel, via telephone, fax, telex, rooftop shouts, and tell-all-over-café-au-lait-tongue-wagging that zipped all over town quicker than all the modern miracles of communication and, *inter alia,* let's not forget the Internet nor short-sell e-mail, which is only a trice slower than the pre-electronic instant mode of communication, you guessed it, it rhymes with e-mail and speaks in a higher-pitched voice and laughs when tickled; or, if the preceding obfuscates rather than clarifies, then let a hint to the wise suffice, so let's not beat around the bush (no offense to the former Prez Pere or junior), we're happy to repeat, let's not forget the Internet, e-mail, and female, which was quicker? hard to say, which is more reliable? let's not play dumb, okay? that Gafni was involved, envalved, invulved with a blonde, full-chested, slim-waisted Polish Catholic shikse exactly half his age, thank God she had a couple of flaws, including pencil-thin eyebrows and vermicelli lips and slightly uneven teeth on an otherwise attractive face, because if she'd been perfect people would have jumped out of their skins, which in any case were already stained a deep envy green, but what Shmulik Gafni, né Weingarten, was thoroughly raked over the coals for was not that he was old enough to be her father (and maybe was), not that she wasn't Jewish (but could become), not that she was Polish, although her Polishness was an awfully bitter pill to swallow (given the Poles' endemic anti-Semitism and how, with few exceptions, they helped the Germans and did no small amount of killing themselves, during and even long after the war, a fact that Gafni knew only too well, and was one of the reasons he went back to Poland so often—about this more, much more, later—but accident of birth wasn't her fault), individually her flaws were excusable and even taken in toto they (that amorphous "they" out there) didn't mind that she was a young, pretty blonde (the fact that she was interested in Jewish history just made them roll their eyes), very busty, how busty? a straining-at-the-sweater busty, a lump-in-the-throat, swallowing-with-difficulty chesty Polish shikse busty, and not even that she was young enough to be his daughter, which we've already mentioned in inverso fashion, but that for God's sake, how could you do this to us, Shmulik Weingarten, because that's who you really are, forget that glib Gafni disguise, Shmulik Weingarten, guardian of Yiddish, laureate of the Yiddish language, faithful amanuensis of Yiddish folklore, editor of Yiddish drama, anthologist and preserver of Yiddish poetry and prose, harvester of Yiddish humor and expert on earthy Yiddish expletives, for God's sake, Shmulik, the blonde bitch, to quote her own surfside confession after the linguistics conference in Nice, a remark that was typed, faxed, whispered, and shouted in all the above-mentioned natural, artificial, and telecommunication modes hitherto listed: the blonde bitch *doesn't even know a word of Yiddish!*

True, Shmulik Gafni didn't want it known all over Jerusalem that he was involved with a Poilishe. Because the truth was—never mind the gossip, the malicious palm-over-mouth sotto voce that went from office to market to bus stop to e-mail to female (quicker than e-mail, see *supra*) but slower than light

(Question: Was there anything that traveled quicker than light? Answer: Yes! Lies!), and what was quicker than lies? Rumors of sex—that he was *not* involved with her. Let's repeat that, given the interruption of long parenthesis and double dashes: he, Shmulik Gafni, was not involved with her. To those skeptics, mockers, and doubters who think Gafni was after Malina (now you know her name) know ye that for years he had dreams that he was not married to Batsheva, but for Gafni they weren't dreams, oh no, they were nightmares in which he felt an awful depression, an emptiness that could only be sensed, never described, an irredeemable loss. In those dreams he was single, alone, lonely, and he felt a discomfit of mysterious origin, a disequilibrium, his wholeness compromised. Salvation came like sunshine breaking suddenly through clouds only when he woke up to find that he was indeed whole, two halves perfectly melded, Batsheva his. Still, there was no doubt in Shmulik's mind and in the minds of others that Malina was an attractive woman. The mystery in the rumor mill was why this lady named Malina Przeskovska (anyone who pronounced her name correctly was assured of her loyalty and friendship and five thousand bonus miles on the other Polish national airline, Less, which had no frequent flyer mileage plan), who already had a PhD in Polish linguistics from Lodz University, was interested in studying Jewish history in Jerusalem. Was it because she had met Gafni at the International Linguistics Conference in Nice and later, as gossip had it, continued their discussions about the niceties and subtleties of comparative linguistics on the finely pebbled beach of Nice where eighty percent of the women were fifty percent naked one hundred percent of the time and the other twenty percent were one hundred percent naked ten percent of the time, engaging in their disquisitions in the international lingua franca (pace, France and French), English?

English? Actually, all this wasn't precisely so. Don't believe all you read, less what you hear, and certainly not what you see.

It began this way.

At the conference Malina gave her paper in English as if she had lived in London for years; actually, she had never set foot either in that country or in the USA. She even took questions in English. So when Gafni approached her in person with a question he didn't want to ask publicly (no, not What's your phone number?) and began at once in Polish, accompanied by his engaging smile, he noticed her surprise, astonishment, pleasure. There was no joy like the joy of hearing your language far away from home, and there was no surprise like the surprise of hearing your native tongue when you did not expect it. She smiled with pleasure at the sound of his words even before she digested the tenor of his remarks. And even as he spoke he saw she was just as pretty up close as she was far away, for beauty at a distance can vanish when blemishes are seen up close.

Gafni studied her face, not for its innate, broad-boned prettiness—she had a large face, with everything in proportion, big eyes and flaring nostrils, which for him was always a sign of womanliness, even overt eroticism, an animal hunger—but also for its air of familiarity.

"Your face looks familiar. I think I've seen it before."

She thought for a moment. "Perhaps at a previous linguistics conference."

"Perhaps," he said. But if so he would have remembered the face and dispensed with that vague ill-at-ease feeling akin to a metaphysical headache. No, he decided, he hadn't seen her at a conference, and the fluttery feeling that her face or a likeness of her face, or a likeness of a likeness, had made an impression on him somewhere remained imprinted on his memory.

Let's get the facts straight. Their chat did not begin on the beach. It began by one of those stone ledges behind the beach, by the promenade. After the conference, when Shmulik still wore jacket and tie and she a business suit, Malina merrily told him she hoped he wouldn't mind if she sunbathed. "I have a bathing suit on under all this," she said in her Polish-accented English, gesturing balletically. Remembering how she brightened when he spoke Polish to her, Gafni courteously suggested speaking Polish, but she, hurt, countered with: "Is my English that poor?" which made him feel bad and prompted him to say that her English was excellent, much better than his, in fact. Gafni confessed that he read English but did not lecture in English. Then wondered aloud if perhaps his unused, perhaps even outmoded, Polish offended her ears. But looking at her made him quickly forget about the language; he only half heard her protestation about his magnificent, literary Polish. Later, upon reflection, Gafni realized that the slow demure striptease she did for him was a kind of non-avian mating dance. She turned modestly and took off her jacket and stepped out of her skirt, rolled down her panty hose, unbuttoned her blouse, still her back to him, doing the sort of undressing gestures done in a hotel room and not on a beach, then, her back still to him, she took out a terrycloth tunic from her bag, put it on, popped her clothes in a plastic bag that emerged from her pocketbook, and lo, she stood before him, turning to face him now, practically naked in her bikini and her nakedness was all the more stark against his full sartorial elegance and she girlishly said to him, taking him by the hand (if indeed she did take his hand and he gave his to her. But if she did extend her hand to him, which still is problematic, and if he took it [even more of a question], if both these suppositions are true and questions of fact, veracity and malicious rumors are resolved and all doubts undone), then

Gafni felt a brief electric thrum in his body, an inexplicable warm jolt that sent a message of no specific linguistic content running in all directions, for she had a firm, assertive clasp that he at once interpreted as goyish, it was a gentile hand clasp, a strong shikse womanly hold, and he followed, seeing and not seeing the half-naked girls sunbathing, even older ones who instead of baring their sagging wrinkled dugs should have covered them in shame with layers of clothing, but even so despite her bikini and the nakedness of the girls on the beach, Gafni felt that she was nakeder than they, it was hard to explain, but if pressed and if he thought about it, the word "sexy" would have come into play, for in the bared breasts there was stasis, nothing provocative or sexy, but in Malina, in that raspberry-colored bikini, Malina bikini, there was something sexy, taking him by the hand for a moment with a flirtatious tilt of her head, "Come to the water," and he followed her, undoing first his tie jerkily as he walked toward the water, left and right, a difficult manipulation when you're working only with one hand, as the whitecaps rolled closer and closer, lapping over the sunning ultramarine sea, the whitecaps breaking here and there like a cupped hand, and then his jacket and shirt, with two hands now, for he thought he'd look funny with only half his jacket and half his shirt off and finally he rolled up his cuffs until at least in spirit, if not in fact, his nakedness matched hers. He didn't realize she'd put his tie into her bag until she'd done it.

"I need sun," Malina sang. "I need sun and light, especially after that gloomy darkness in the lecture halls." And she removed her little terrycloth tunic.

Shmulik remembered reading once in an American novel a description of a woman with a "luscious body," and he recalled the phrase perhaps because the first syllable of "luscious"—lush—was the first syllable too of *loshn*, the Yiddish word for "tongue" and "language," and he repeated to himself, "What a luscious body."

Heads turned when Malina took off her terrycloth tunic and the sun shone on her deep raspberry red bikini top. Traffic stopped. The Nice-Monte Carlo helicopter shuttle hovered in midair. Storks carrying babies on their way over the Alps to nest in Morocco's Atlas Mountains swooped down, leaving some half-dozen Eskimo tykes homeless. For a moment Shmulik was blinded by the size, shape, pitch, timbre, mode, and musicality of the large ripe Galilee melons, first image that came to his Israeli mind, recalling the stacks of melons in the Jerusalem outdoor market, fruits that were popping out of their baskets, so small were the restraints—we're back to Malina's melons now—so large the countervailing force. And all this in contrast to her slim waist. Women of intellect weren't supposed to have bodies like that, Gafni thought, rubbing the sunlight from his eyes. His *loshn* cleaved to the roof of his mouth, as the phrase in the Psalms had it ("If I forget thee, O Jerusalem, may my tongue cleave to the roof of my mouth"), and even though he hadn't forgotten Jerusalem he was, temporarily, as the Yiddish proverb had it: *un loshn*, without tongue, or speechless.

He swallowed, although swallowing was difficult, what with his tongue stuck up there somewhere on his palate (I guess he *had* forgotten Jerusalem), and the everlasting springs of spittle as dry as the Negev desert in August. Temptation was like a snake slithering in the grass, ready to strike, then retreating into serpentine slumber: temptation flashed its venomous wet fangs. Temptation, blood-filled, pounded its hammers on both sides of Shmulik's head, no syncopation here, rather perfectly timed right and left. He looked away, looked to the calm blue sea; tried to breathe in the blue of the water, the azure of the sky. In the lecture hall he had seen her in a business suit where she wasn't exactly flat-chested, but he attributed some of the fullness to the cut of the jacket. He couldn't imagine then that he would see later what he was seeing now.

Rather than say something stupid, he sought to steer the conversation back to linguistics. In such situations, *loshn* (hope you haven't forgotten, *loshn*, like *lingua* in Italian, means both "tongue" and "language") always comes in handy.

"Do you know what your name means in Yiddish?"

"No. I don't know. I don't even know one word of Yiddish," she said apologetically, but with a seductive little tilt of her head. The slight musical whine of her words declared: Teach me. I'm willing to learn.

"It means 'berry.'"

"Ah," Malina brightened. "Also in Polish and Russian."

"Yes, of course."

She frowned. "How could it be the same in Yiddish and Polish?"

How could "telephone" be the same in Russian, Yiddish, Polish, English, Dutch, Swahili, and Hebrew? he was about to lecture her, but then supposed it was a purposely naïve question, a come-on. She had a degree in linguistics, for goodness sake. Surely she knew.

So without condescension he told her, "Because Yiddish has influences from many language groupings, including Slavic."

And so all these rumors of "what was known all over Jerusalem" ("I mean, you know," folks would say, "it's known all over town.") were utter and absolute nonsense. They were colleagues and friends, Malina and Shmulik. She said she had always had a fascination with Jewish history, like many of her post-War-born, intellectually minded friends. And since there were advanced fellowships available, it wasn't hard for Malina, that pretty little berry—once her name became known, it was the subject of a whole series of, God preserve us, fruity jocular concoctions—to get admitted to the Jewish history graduate program for a second PhD at the University of Israel. And guess who was helping her with beginners' Hebrew and Yiddish?

We think you also ought to know that Shmulik's Batsheva was not well. She was ailing, in fact, at home, diabetic, and Shmulik would not compromise his affection for his wife by carrying on with another woman, luscious very berry though she was. In fact, Gafni hadn't wanted to go to the Nice Conference, but Batsheva urged him to go. You were looking forward to this trip, she said. Go to Nice. Don't worry. I'll be all right.

Strange. In short, Gafni went to Nice. If he hadn't gone, he wouldn't have met Malina and the rumors would not have begun. But Malina or no Malina, with Gafni there was always room for gossip.

He knew of course that women looked admiringly at him. Although he was not tall, he was of robust appearance, solidly built, no flab. He swam, he could walk backwards quicker than most people could walk forward, played tennis in a city that hadn't developed the sport, even skied when he went to winter conferences in Switzerland. His grandfather lived to his ninety-third birthday; his father would have too, had he not been murdered by *them*. So the chances were good for Shmulik Gafni too and he worked hard on his longevity.

And, of course, his mental acuity matched—what do you mean "matched"? It easily surpassed—his physical vigor. By the age of seventy, when he had been awarded Israel's highest honor, the Israel Prize, for his life's work, presented at the President of Israel's residence, Shmulik had already won the Bialik Prize for his study of Alsatian Yiddish; the Tel Aviv Prize for his book on nineteenth-century Yiddish in Jerusalem; and an honorary doctorate from Oxford for his edition of the collected works of a hitherto unknown sixteenth-century Venetian master of Yiddish. In addition, among his one hundred-eleven books and monographs, there was a rather slim anthology of Yiddish jokes in Sicily; an edition of neglected twentieth-century Yiddish writers in Albania and Herzegovina; a study of early Swiss variants of the verb "to be," which he proved were derivatives of Old Yiddish.

Gafni's Latin-Yiddish, Yiddish-Latin dictionary was a tour de force. And his Latin translation of one of Sholom Aleichem's comic monologues was the hit of the International Latin Scholars Conference, the famous ILSC, held on Capri, for Latin conventions, like Yiddish conferences, always chose perfect locations and ideal weather for their week-long *festa festorae*. It put Yiddish on the map. When Gafni quotes Cicero's "A room without books is like a body without a soul" in his Yiddish—"*a tzimmer un a sefer is azoy vi a guf un a neshomeh*"—it sounds natural, homey, heimish. You would have thought Cicero grew up in a shtetl, and perhaps he did.

Of course, such productivity and fame sparked envy, and envy gave birth to criticism that soon degenerated to petty carping. (You see what I mean. Malina or no Malina, the carps are always there to nibble and quibble.) They criticized Gafni for his frequent trips abroad (trips they'd rather have taken). Why can't he stay home and teach? They skewered him for publishing so much. Why didn't we think of this first? Why doesn't he rein in his pen (creating in their envy a mixed metaphor)? Why doesn't he get writer's block, writer's cramp? Why does he dance all over the globe? Sicily, Alsace-Lorraine, Switzerland, Tirana, Shanghai. Next thing we know he'll be writing about Yiddish in Timbuktu. (Which, incidentally, he was working on already.)

Again lies and malignation. He did stay home and teach. But the carps would not cease nibbling, the piranhas their petty carping: Why did he, that is Shmulik Gafni, always manage to find a Yiddish connection in world-class resorts? No one else but pleasure-garden-seeking, wine-bibbing Weingarten; no one but globe-hopping Gafni could find Yiddish in the Canary Islands, the Azores, Palma di Majorca, or Malta, where the last Yiddish speaker had died peacefully in his sleep in the year twenty-two of the Common Era, a total, unwarranted exaggeration. And what possible link could there be between Yiddish, continued the carpers, or anything remotely Jewish for that matter, and the Taj Mahal, yet Gafni was able to come up with an article only semi-tongue-in-cheek entitled, "The Taj Mahal, the Pink Elephant, and the Jewish Question." Success breeds envy, period. What next, Gafni? Yiddish in Yemen? Jargon in Azerbaijan? *Mame-loshn* in Mozambique?

But how about fairness, balance, eh? That's the Jewish way. His students thought he was a gifted instructor. His teaching assistants adored him. He always took one or two along and managed to find international grants and fellowships for them. And ask the members of the various Polish *landsmanshaftn* in Israel how often Shmulik would appear before their groups and reminisce with them about pre-war Jewish life in Warsaw and other cities and never charge a lecturer's fee.

Given all of the above, it is no wonder that Shmulik Gafni did not want known all over Jerusalem what was known all over Jerusalem, a so-called "known" that, according to Gafni, had no connection to fact, but facts, as is well known, no quotes around *that* word, facts had as much connection to truth as cabbies to cabbage or cribs to cribbage. You've heard this before, but a truism—like a juicy lie—is worth repeating (in fact, Gafni himself liked to use this line and would ascribe it to various eighteenth-century *philosophes*): a truism, like a lie, gets better with each repetition. Mere fact, mere access to truth, did not prevent lies from growing like a golem out of control.

The truth was that Shmulik Gafni was never alone with Malina. Giving her an occasional lift home in his car—a six-minute ride—to save her a forty-minute bus ride does not count. He drove; she sat next to him. Gafni looked down at her short skirt and bare, pretty legs and in his mind he stretched out his hands and touched, stroked her smooth, tanned skin, a tan and a bare that reminded him of the tan and the bare when he walked with her on the Nice beach to the water of the Great Sea, as the Bible called the blue Mediterranean, and even though she was partially clothed then she was nakeder than the ninety-eight percent naked women on the beach. But all this was in his head; his hands on his lap he kept (and if I were Chaucer I would add: and Shmulik Gafni was he yclept). Looking at his calm hands and tranquil fingers, one would never have imagined the tremble in his fingers, the quake in his heart, the shake in his soul, the *agitas* in all of Gafni.

So then, Gafni was never really alone with Malina. Even when he traveled with his assistants, male and female, he never stayed at the same hotel with them. Of course, when he was invited by various conferences, he was always lodged in the best hotel, which perk, alas, could not be offered to his assistants. And even when by pure coincidence Malina registered (who her sponsor was no one knew) for the same conference, she always stayed at a different hotel.

But this didn't satisfy them (the "them" out there previously cited as "they"). They figured that precisely, *davke*, *because* the two of them were in different hotels it actually confirmed their suspicions. Why different hotels? Just *because* it's different hotels, they argued Talmudically, was all the more reason to believe that something was going on. It was such a transparent ruse, that different-hotels ploy (there's that "ploy" again), even more revealing than if they'd been in the same hotel. Who are they (a different "they" this time) fooling with that two-hotels monkey business? If vox populi makes up its mind, even truth can't come to interfere, as Cicero sagely observed.

And so with this—we now paraphrase a remark in one of Kafka's meta-fictions—we have come to the end of our investigation as to what was known (remember Pascal's apothegm: all knowledge is either Platonic arrogance or wishful thought) and not known in the holy city of Jerusalem, may it speedily be rebuilt in our day, Amen, by presenting all the facts as we know them.

MOONCAKE

My friendship with Mordy Moscowitz was based on a lively mutual animosity that non—New Yorkers could never appreciate or comprehend. We always spoke as if people were watching us debating, and mentally kept score of points if we got in a particularly devastating thrust. It was the only game in the world that pleased both winner and loser. Among the things I could not stand in Mordy, my pal and sparring partner since 1-A, was that he had never left New York. I don't mean the physical limits of New York City, for New York City is a state of mind, a metaphysical presence, which for Mordy meant warmth, tribal security, homeland. Whether in Miami Beach during our freshman intersession, or up in the Borscht Belt to wait on tables in the summer—small and quick, he could lift heavy trays and remember a dozen different egg orders with ease—or at a weekend in Tanglewood (Menuhin playing Bloch, Steinberg conducting Gershwin and Copland), Mordy never left his NYC of the imagination.

Mordy feared the vast goyland that stretched beyond his gerrymandered New York. Lynchings scared him. Pogroms in an America shifting slowly to the right. The WASPs—professors didn't count—overwhelmed him. I don't know if he spoke to six in his life. For Mordy Moscowitz, a guy who had never experienced anti-Semitism, it *could* happen here.

That's why I hesitated telling him directly about our forthcoming trip. To break the news gently, I got a map of the U.S. and pasted little golden stars on all the major Jewish urban centers.

"Your biblical cities of refuge," I said, unfurling the map.

Adjusting his glasses, he poked his nose into the map and—so help me—sniffed it, as if testing the pastrami in Memphis Louie's Kosher Deli. His hesitant fingers skimmed along the magic carpet flecked with gold.

"Six glorious weeks," I said. "Cross-country. The charm of America. Girls. Sleeping bags. Starlight. Girls by moonlight. Girls in sleeping bags."

"You sure they won't kill us, Sam?"

"Who, the girls? Maybe you they'll kill. Me, I'm an iron horse."

"No. I mean the Others. Everygoy. The United anti-Semites of America, Incorporated. They hear my Brooklyn accent in a state park down south and we're finished."

"Don't worry. We'll go fifty-fifty on gas, oil, and all repairs."

Mordy's maniacal laugh. "I suspected a commercial sooner or later. I should repair your jalopy?"

"I should be your private chauffeur twelve hours a day? I should shlep to Frisco one of the few guys in America who can't drive a car?"

"All right, crook, fifty-fifty."

"But as a consolation prize, my mother is going to bake—"

"Oh no, not again!"

"—an extra special gigantic poppyseed *mohn-cak*e for you. Every bite in Virginia, Tennessee, and Texas will bring back memories of New York. If it won't fit into the trunk, we'll—"

"Leave it home?"

"—put it on the roof rack."

A week later we were ready to go. I brought my cake, and Mordy filled the rest of the trunk with three of the fattest novels in print: *Kristin Lavransdatter*, *Anna Karenina, and Jean Christophe*. He was in high spirits until we crossed the Mason-Dixon line. But at the sight of wisteria trees and Spanish moss he grew edgy. Hearing Southern accents he clammed up. I had to order gas in filling stations and food in diners. He groaned when he saw an occasional Jewish name on stores that whizzed by, and sympathized with the poor guy's eventual doom. He complained about the repair bills, and, worse, deflated my erotic fantasies of nymphos in the woods.

I hummed to myself as I drove; then, looking straight ahead, announced: "I promise to be patient from now on with Mordy Moscowitz and other pests."

"And I, in turn, affirm that henceforth I will treat Sam Bergerman and other auto thieves with the kindness reserved for dogs and other dumb creatures."

After sunset we found a state park. We pulled into a campsite at twilight and began preparing our sleeping bags. The darkness swooped over us like a black umbrella. I switched on my flash-light, undressed, and, exhausted from the long drive, slipped into my sack.

"I hear water running," Mordy said. "I'll be right back."

Mordy followed the light of the trailer and sounds of a well being pumped. Two minutes later he was back, shaking me by the shoulders.

"Jeesuz Cur-rist! I just saw a mermaid with legs, washing dishes by the pump. Seventeen, eighteen. In a bathing suit. Pair of boobs like Sophia Loren. You never saw anything like it in your life."

"Has she got a friend for you?"

Mordy pressed his glasses to his nose and cackled. "I'll give you friend. I found her."

"Did you talk to her?"

"Not yet. I mean—"

"And you shlep Tolstoy with you. Books wherever you go that you never read. Life, man, life. Use your mouth. Your hands."

"Yeah, man, yeah." Mordy rubbed his hands.

"But you got to talk to them before you touch them. Ask her what time it is. Then if there's swimming around here. Then how long she plans to stay."

"Time. Swimming. Stay," Mordy mumbled, turned, and walked back.

I scrambled out of the sleeping bag and caught Mordy by the arm. "I'll give you Time, Swimming, Stay, you sneaky bastard. You're not cashing in on my line."

"I saw her first. Hey, where are you going, Sam? You got your underwear on."

I came back and slipped into my pants and shoes. Took a glass and crashed through the bushes, like a moth following light, until I came to the pump. I aimed my glance at the pump, but sensed she was there, somewhere out of my range of vision, within another more subtle periphery.

"Hi," I said, turning as though just noticing her.

"Hi, yourself," she said.

That bright red two-piece bathing suit danced like a light on my retina even after I had turned to the well. I pumped the handle, holding my glass under the nozzle. The water overflowed the glass, good and cold. I sipped, peeking over the rim at her.

Time. Swimming. Stay. "Do—"

"Do you know what time it is?" she said, stepping up to the pump with some dishes.

"About nine or so, I guess."

"I'll bet you're surprised to see me in a bathing suit at night."

"Not at all. In fact, I would've been more surprised if you *hadn't* been wearing a bathing suit."

"You mean," she gestured at her body, "stark raving nude? Naked?"

I felt my face getting red. "I mean, if instead of a bathing suit, you'd have been dressed regular-like."

"Well, I just love swimming by moonlight."

On the movie screen of my mind flashed three magic titles.

"How lo—" I began.

"We've been here for three days and we love it here. Golly, I never want to go home. How long you planning to stay?" She bent down toward the handle, but I grabbed it and began pumping. As I watched the beautiful twilight cleavage of her breasts, those horses seeking exit from the red cloth cage, the water spurted out of the nozzle.

Then I looked at her fingers and my heart fell. Not because of the red dishpan hands that marred her beauty. But because of the thick golden wedding band on her left ring finger.

"I'm leaving tomorrow morning," I backed away. "We're just here for the night, me and my buddy."

The girl smiled; a warm, married-woman smile, full of matronly kindliness that says, "I'd love to give you what you want but my husband won't let me." A smile packed with the confidence of her warm bed and my cold lonely sack. I turned, mumbled goodnight, stumbled through the bushes to our campsite. At least she's got dishpan hands. Nobody's perfect.

"Shit," I said, kicking one of my tires. "She's married. She's got a ring on her finger."

"Good. Serves you right. This is the happiest moment of my life."

I pulled off my shoes and crawled back into the sleeping bag without getting undressed. My thoughts thrummed like telephone wires; I pictured the placid Shenandoah Valley, world's longest picture postcard. I couldn't relax. I looked up at the full moon sailing through the clouds. The wind was changing. I closed my eyes, trying to enjoy the clean pine air. Felt zipped in, closed in, trapped. Here I was in a sleeping bag while my imagination skirted around the pump where the trailer light was still shining. What's she doing out there, KP for a platoon? I breathed deeply; the air rasped the back of my throat. I could use a drink. A glass of cold water.

Softly, I eased the zipper down, got out, stepped into my shoes. Moscowitz was a heavy sleeper, but no sense giving explanations. Began tiptoeing away, knowing it was too good to be true.

"The ring's still on her finger." Clear and sleepless. "Where you going?"

"In the morning you can't wake him. All of a sudden he's Cerberus with a thousand eyes. I'm going for a drink."

I waited. Mordy didn't say a word. "May I take ten giant steps? Thanks a lot. Were you asleep, Moscowitz?"

"Out here it's Mordy, okay?"

"What's bugging *you*?"

"Can't sleep. The chick's given me hot pants," Mordy said.

"I'll bring you back some ice water to douse your passion. Meanwhile, whack off to your heart's content."

I ran over to the pump. She was still there, puttering around, putting the finishing touches to the dishes. I noticed a little table set for three. A baby to boot. How cozy; maybe she'd whip out a snapshot.

"Hi, again." She smiled. "Thirsty?"

"Driving all day makes me thirsty. I could drink like a camel."

"You can have the pump in just a sec. Just let me fill this pitcher."

"Here, let me."

I looked at her hand again; like a moth to flame my eyes went for her ring finger. But now my heart came up from my feet and zoomed through the top of my skull into outer space, the first human heart in orbit. The ring was no marriage ring at all, but a plain old high school ring which she had evidently turned around while washing.

"We also get pooped driving all day long. The minute we get into a park Daddy and Mother go right to bed. It's their vacation. They can sleep around the clock I bet. Me, I got so much energy I can get along on an hour's sleep. I keep busy 'cause I got to work off energy."

"I got some excess energy of my own I'd like to work off. How about a moonlight swim? You can lead me to the lake, which I don't even know where it is."

"Sure thing. Wait a sec 'til I get a towel."

Heart back in my mouth, I wondered if she would return. When she came back I offered her my hand.

"Let's trot," I said as we walked down the path. "I can't wait to get in the water."

"Me too," said Moscowitz.

"Oh," the girl shrieked and leaned into my chest. Her breast dug into my ribs. I put a protective arm around her and thought of the stories I'd tell back home of the mermaid in the park.

"Don't worry, it's only my lonely roommate. Where you headed, Mordy? I thought your trousers were on fire."

"Oh my! I can get you one of Daddy's dungarees if you like," she said.

"Why don't you introduce us, Sam?" Mordy said.

"Okay. Meet my buddy and long-time nemesis, Mordy Mosc—"

"Moscow. Mordy Moscow. And your name is Mrs.—?"

She giggled. "He's cute. My name's Ginny. Back home they call me Bunny."

"I thought you were m—"

"Ixnay uckshmay," I pulled Mordy's arm as I gave him a dose of Pig Latin. "Conference. Excuse me a minute, Bunny." I led Mordy behind a tree. "What's this Mordy Moscow bit?" I whispered. "Ashamed?"

"Not at all. But you got to be careful."

"Better red than dead."

I ran back to Ginny and whispered in her ear, "Would you like some mooncake?"

"What's that?"

"Sweets from the moon. Ambrosia."

"Sounds great," she said. "Love to."

Mordy followed me back to the car. "Scram, bastard," I hissed. I opened the trunk and sliced off a couple of hunks of cake.

"You want to poison her?" he said.

"Clear off. Can't you see I've got a good thing going?"

"I saw her first. Fifty-fifty."

Bunny ate the mooncake and, despite Mordy's warnings, loved it. I did too, especially when I fed her and her lips nibbled my fingers on the last bite. We sat quietly, all three of us, staring at the faintly stirring dark green lake, which lapped broken moonbeams at the shoreline. Once in a while a fish plopped up for air. I looked at Bunny. Closed my eyes. When I reopened them she was still there. So was Moscowitz.

"You like music, Bunny?"

"Love it."

"Here's a game we like to play back home in Brooklyn. I whistle a tune in your ear. Listen." I put my lips up to her ear, held the hair away and whistled "Blue Moon."

"Quit it," she laughed, wriggling around. "It tickles."

"You got to get used to it," I insisted. And whistled some more. "Now. Name the tune."

"'Blue Moon' . . . hey, that rhymes," she giggled. "Do I get a prize?"

"Yes." I kissed her ear.

"And now, Mordy Moscowitz, secret agent, will take a moonlight dip in the lake and show us how long he can stay under."

"Not when 'Blue Moon' is on," Mordy said. "My own personal anthem."

"In that case, I'm going to whistle the tune he hates the most. 'Blue Mooncake.' This song is dedicated to Mordy Moscow, who like Hamlet left his witz back home."

I whistled, and she crinkled her nose, shuddering.

"All right, miss." I faked a show biz style. "Name . . . The . . . Tune!"

"'Blue Mooncake'?"

"Right you are. And so you get another kiss."

"Hey, there's nothing that cool back home in Bath."

"Where's that?"

"Ohio."

"Cool . . . bath . . . Get it, Bunny? Cool . . . Bath," Mordy said and roared with laughter.

"There's nothing more miserable than laughing alone, is there Mordy?"

"Oh, that's not nice," Bunny said. "It *was* funny."

Mordy threw pebbles into the water.

"Want to hear another tune, Bunny?" I asked.

"Love to."

"And now something with a Latin BEAT," I said. Behind Bunny's back I mimed "IT" to Mordy who got the message but satanically shook his head. The moon, two of them, glinted in his glasses. Italian style, he slammed his left palm into his right muscle and swung a fierce fungoo at me.

"You want to hear it in Anglo-Saxon now?" Mordy said.

"I'll tell you a secret why I'm traveling with Mordy," I whispered into Bunny's ear, blew into it as though to test a microphone, and since—what not?—I was already there, nibbled a bit. "My friend is a sex maniac. Doctors recommended Frisco. They say he'll recover his witz there. So I'm taking him to an institution on the coast. Over."

She whispered back, her lips on my ear. "Is he dangerous? Over."

"More moonstruck than dangerous," I whispered back and kissed her ear. "Notice how he wouldn't join us in the mooncake rites. That's his hangup. Anything with the moon. Moonmaniac. Or as they say in Latin—*lunaticus maniacus*. Want to take a walk?"

"Love to."

We got up holding hands.

"Me too" Mordy stood.

"Conference."

I pulled Mordy behind a tree again, not joking this time. "Tonight, Moscow," I seethed, "you're gonna wake up with your throat slit from ear to ear. Enough's enough, you putz."

"Okay by me, shmuck, but what'll you do tomorrow night?"

"Leave you flat. Pull out alone. See if I don't, Mordy. So beat it pal and there'll be peace 'til Frisco."

"Peace me no peace. I want a piece of the action. Now. I found her. She's mine. Fifty-fifty. Including repairs."

"Fuck you."

I turned, walked back to Bunny, and took her hand. Even in the dark I felt the rough redness of her fingers. Poor Cinderella. Did she have to do the dishes all the time?

"Let's take this path." I put my arm around her waist.

Mordy tagged along, hopping on the long shadows.

"Do you think I'm pretty?" she said.

"Pretty? You're beautiful! You're so beautiful I'm going to dance with you!"

"No music," Bunny said.

"Who needs music? We'll whistle. A tango. Da dada *tee* tum, dada *tee* tum, dada *tee* tum."

Taking large slow steps, I backed away from Mordy and pressed Bunny close to me.

"Golly, this is fun. I never had so much fun in Bath. All we do out there is the same old thing. Book in the drive-ins."

"What's that?"

"Don't you know what booking is?"

"I know what making book is."

"It's kissing, silly. Fooling around. What do you call it back home?"

"Back in Brooklyn we call it making out."

"And we call it booking."

"It shows high culture. Like this?" I kissed her lower lip. It tasted bittersweet, ammoniac, the kisses like moonbeams mixed with buttermilk. She closed her eyes. As I came in for a close-up like a screen lover, I saw Mordy standing in the moonlight alone, watching. With one hand I waved him away.

He responded with sign language of different vintage, then came running up, his tongue hanging out. "The Bible says, 'Of making book there is no end.' So mind if I cut in?"

"Only if you turn the other cheek."

"May I have this dance?" Mordy said.

"With pleasure," I said, taking his hand and going into some steps.

He shoved me away. "Bunny?"

"Sure," she said.

"Remember the moon," I warned.

Mordy put his arm around her and moved in.

"Un-uh," Bunny said. "Watch me. Put your arms behind your back. With you I'm going to square dance."

"Why square dance?" Mordy whined.

"Because you're a red square, Moscow," I said.

"All right, I get the hint," Mordy said. "I see I'm not wanted. I'll go if you make a deal with me."

I bowed orientally. "Your conditions?" I said, tightlipped.

"First get rid of the mooncake. Second, I just want a little page from a book, one kiss from a pretty miss."

"I agree to the first condition," I said. "Anything for peace. The second you'll have to negotiate with Bunny. I'm not her lawyer."

"I don't know," Bunny said. "What should I do? He's cute."

"Conference."

This time I pulled Bunny away. "Listen, I got a terrific idea. Tell him yes, but when he's about to kiss you, just before he does, whisper to him: 'Would you like to come into my trailer with me and help my father and me plan a pogrom?'"

"But I don't *want* him to come into my trailer."

"Don't worry, sweetie. Trust me. Repeat after me: Would you like to come into my trailer with me and help my father and me plan a pogrom?"

"Would you like to come into my trailer with me and help my father and me plan a pogrom? How's that?"

"Great."

"What's a pogrom?"

"A party, like. Real swinging. Which a square like him despises. Just see what happens."

We walked back to Mordy. "All right, you win. She's willing."

As Mordy closed in for the kill, she said, "Wait, I want to tell you something," and whispered her line grandly.

She didn't even finish the key word when Mordy, with a yelp of pain, stung and loco, wrenched out of her grasp and made for the bushes, crashing his way back to the campsite.

I whistled "In Loveland for Me and My Gal" and stepped off the path onto the grass. We sat down, kissed, and I gently eased her back down.

"Listen to the darkness," I said, not knowing whether to enjoy the moment or the memory of it already coalescing in my mind. "Isn't it beautiful? You can hear the trees breathing."

"It makes you think," she said, rubbing my neck.

"Wife of Bath, I'd like to shower you with kisses," I said. "You're beautiful."

"No I'm not either. I've got ugly hands."

"No." I took her hands and kissed them.

"I tried wearing rubber gloves, but it still don't help. They're sensitive to everything."

"You're lovely all over."

"I like booking with you. You're swell. You're different."

"I've always liked books myself. My moonstricken friend, poor guy, he's only after sex and skin. For instance, take me, I never judge a book by its cover," I said, working on her halter. "It's the contents that impress me. Did you ever read a book by Braille? Greatest author in the world."

"You're funny."

Somewhere a car was starting, sputtering, dying, then starting again. It made me nervous. Spoiled my reading. The headlights swerved through the trees, away, then curved a U-turn down the road. We crawled back into the high grass. The car passed, then idled about twenty feet ahead of us.

"It stopped," I said. "Is it your father?"

Bunny quickly scrambled for her halter and snapped it on. "Can't be. He's asleep. And anyway he doesn't have an old dark-looking car. Think it's the park police? We're not doing anything wrong, are we?"

"North Carolina is a sovereign state," I assured her.

"Thank goodness. I feel better already."

"What the hell! It's my car." I ran to it and the car bumped forward again. "Hey, you, who's in my car?"

"It's me," Mordy shouted from the driver's seat. "Don't come any closer. Take one step, either of you, and away I zoom. I got a good mind to leave you here, Sam, but I feel sorry for you, so I'll let you in on a little secret."

"What's your secret?" I shouted. "That you can't drive? Day and night I drive and all—"

"When I'm mad I learn quick. Watch this," and spurted ahead another fifteen feet.

"You leaving? Now?" Bunny whispered, the tears starting in her eyes.

"He's stealing my car. He'll kill himself. My best friend, the nut."

She threw her arms around me and kissed me. "Goodnight, Sam. You're the cutest craziest guy in the whole USA." She turned and ran back into the woods.

"Wait," I shouted. What am I doing? The hell with the car, the hell with Mordy Moscowitz, my albatross for fifteen years. "Wait!" But another forward roar of the motor drowned my cry.

I turned this way and that. The two things I loved most in the world—Bunny and my car—were fast disappearing in opposite directions. Cursing my luck, I ran to the car, caught up to it.

"You bastard!"

"Come in," Mordy said. "For God's sake, quick. It's a matter of life or death."

Frightened, I got into the car. Mordy was wheezing, breathing strangely. He looked green around the gills. There was an unearthly moonstruck gleam on his face. I conjured up pictures of hospitals, specialists, oxygen tanks, and was figuring how much half of that would cost me. Hell, I thought, I'm not Blue Cross. The fifty-fifty deal is only for transportation, not Medicare.

"There's a pogrom a-brewing," Mordy said. "I was right after all."

"My God," I shouted, suddenly inspired, realizing that the moment just lost might be recaptured. "Quick," I pointed. "Over there. That light."

As Mordy turned, I dived forward—Mordy too: too late—and in one quick motion grabbed the key and shut the motor. "Got you now."

"Who's got who?" Mordy grinned. "It's the name of a brand new parlor game."

He leaned back and closed his eyes.

"Moonstruck I am. Mooncake I become," he said.

I pressed the key into my fist, deciding what to do.

The noises of the night, wrapped in silence, waved into the car. In the distance, we heard the pogrom's first victim, crying her eyes out.

THE METAMORPHOSIS OF FREDDY COLE

"Three rungs to the ladder: contemplation, words to the heart, action."

—Buddhist proverb

"What I want is less talk and more action."

—Fred Cole, diary entry

When Fred Cole first saw her through the windshield, he knew he was in love again. She sat cross-legged on a flat rock just outside the landscaped entrance to the campus, thumb up and hitching, her long sun-gleaming hair hanging over her eyes, the wind wisping the strands just as in slick fiction. Hooked, Fred gazed at the blonde and realized she was number one hundred what? in an endless list of loves who passed into one door of his life and out the other with slapstick-film rapidity. They snapped out of buses, crackled behind signs, popped around corners—but they never stopped for him.

Fred looked up at the rearview mirror. Another image gliding out of his life forever—and adjusted the mirror to wipe the memory away. He parked at the college bookstore lot, showed the manager the new texts his firm was publishing, and, as casually as he could, hurried away. The back of his neck felt hot with discomfort—conscience coming out in flushes of heat—at the injustice he'd done to Boston Books. Poor firm, it paid a horny twenty-six-year-old salesman to sell and promote its books.

In the car again, he rushed to see the girl but realized that the girl would not, could not possibly, be there. Blonde and attractive, nubile thumb out and seductive, the only thing he'd ever see of her again was the impression she'd made on his mind. The minute she slid out of his mirror she obviously slid onto the back seat of some motorcyclist long on hair and luck. He soared over the last hill, stomach dipping as though on a huge swing with eyes closed, courting vertigo. At the entrance, he applied the brakes slowly. First to the car, then to his heart, not believing his luck. She stood, squinted at him.

"Cambridge?"

Cole nodded, though his destination, next business call in fact, was Wellesley, exactly one hundred-eighty degrees away. He observed her through the trick mirror curve in his windshield. Long baby face, sad eyes and pouting lips. The brown eyes spoke he knew not what, and he was spellbound by the hair netting like some rare lace across the plexiglass.

With long confident strides she went around to the door, entered, and pressed the lock button. She had two fat paperbacks in her hand, *Tom Jones* by Fielding and another he could not see. It rang some vague bell from a long gone lit class, and for a moment—evanesced before he could savor it—recalled the timeless zone of college days. Was it for a course? He wanted to ask. In reply, she quickly—quite furtively, he thought—folded them into her big pocketbook. The hot flush on the back of his neck returned. Again the firm riding on his back. And he, driving to Cambridge, on company time. Why had Boston Books suddenly filled, invaded his thoughts, if he was thinking about the girl now, looking at her legs, her lap, her bag? Her books. With his firm's trademark, two super-imposed B's. Two B's rising out of the books hidden in her bag, climbing onto his back, a paper albatross soaring from the object of his guilt.

Not knowing what to say, Fred reveled in his good fortune. What more could a guy ask for? Doll-like, she radiated the innocent sweetness that was his ideal, like the girl in the soda pop ad, clothed in a toga, sitting in a rock, legs dipping into a half-seen pool. He breathed deeply. Tried to assess the increasing closeness in the car. Was it within him? Or simply the silence, uncomfortably warm? Actually, the more one got used to it, the easier it was to maintain. Fred Cole liked her silence, the way she cooperated in that spur of the moment project to remain still. It was better, more intimate, somehow, than love.

Turning to see if she was still there, he saw her almost at his side, inches away. So, the special frequency that he believed existed between him and certain girls was working. Thank God for biochemistry. He looked at her, but she stared out at the Charles River with a dreamy cuddled expression. Isn't a girl like you afraid to hitch?

Three blocks away from Harvard Square, she said, "Here we are," and pointed to a third-story window where another blonde, with short-cropped hair, was waving down to her. Cole noted the address.

Don't tell me, he didn't say. I know. It's your apartment.

Gazing past her hair, he mesmerized a rope ladder up to the window, hand over heart following his thoughts inside, and choked up with the wonderful mysteries of privacy that it contained.

She got out. "Thanks a lot, mister." Slammed the door.

The name's Fred Cole, he didn't say, so don't call me Mister. How about taking a ride with me up to North Country tomorrow?

Don't be late, was her reply.

On the highway west he began speeding, his heart now at the tip of the hood. When he stopped for gas, he slipped his hand into his right hand jacket pocket and discovered, instead of three dollars, that he'd been robbed.

The next day at 3 p.m. Cole again waited at the entrance to the campus, watching the rock, recreating his fantasy on it. Ten minutes passed, fifteen, twenty. He drove away, looking at the rearview mirror, last hope he'd see her coming. Then he remembered the odd combination of college class schedules. Wednesday and Thursday didn't match. But Wednesday and Friday did. On Friday he drove back and forth in front of the campus, his heart a tom-tom in his torso. Then he saw her striding to the hitching point with her long-legged languid pace.

"Want a ride?" he said softly, against his will.

She narrowed her eyes at him, smiled in recognition. No hint of guilt or shame. Perhaps she hadn't done it after all. She rose, tucked a few books under her arm, and got into the car.

"What are you doing here?"

"Business."

A frown of disbelief.

"And pleasure," he added

"Well, at least you can talk."

"And walk, and sing, too . . . Cambridge?"

She nodded. "How come you didn't say a word the other day?"

"Well . . ."

"It was quite impressive, I must say. Not hearing small talk and silly questions for a change."

Huddled to the door, she gazed out the rear window, then suddenly hunched down in her seat.

"What's up?" Fred asked.

"Cops. Following," she said, turning again.

"No trouble," said Cole. "I'm not speeding." He felt for his wallet, now secure in his left breast pocket.

"It's campus patrol. They're af—"

"Wait a minute! Campus police can't stop me. They've got no authority beyond campus."

"Are you sure?"

"Of course I'm Sure. Watch." He pulled to the right lane, eased up on the accelerator. The car overtook them.

"See?"

"Uhuh."

Look, he didn't say. *How about going out?*, he didn't ask.

He drove for a while, rehearsing the question. The speedometer rose and fell, like his heartbeats, and his nerve. Telephone poles faded by. No time to lose. If he waited any longer, nothing would remain of the question except an unsaid question mark.

"Would you like to take a ride with me tomorrow? Up to the North Country?"

"Saturday is no good. Saturdays I model. . . . Take this exit. Bear right. Do you know your way from here?"

"Sure. . . . Where do you model?"

"For an art class."

"Not nude?"

"Oh yes. Naked. Absolutely."

He pulled up in front of her house, his fingers plugging the holes in his heart. "Naked?"

"Where else could I make easy bucks?"

Pickpocketing me, he didn't say.

"Want to see me model?"

No! Fred didn't shout.

He looked at her closely. Saw a baby face framed with dark golden hair, a slightly jutting chin and lower lip that gave her, when she smiled, an elfish grin. Her eyes blinked slowly, distantly, as though trying to conjure up a thought just beyond reach. She looked as if she was either nearsighted or was just getting used to contact lenses. Expressions swiftly moving—chagrin and surprise, mingling with disbelief.

"No thanks," Cole said. "It would spoil it. Understand?"

"Will you come visit me?"

He hesitated, not purposely, long enough to see her eyes pleading. And then noticed the carefully powdered indented rings under her eyes, her attempt to hide the harrowed look of someone who had just staggered, with dignity, out of a pleasure dome.

"How's tomorrow night?"

"I'm entertaining my cousin. He'll be in from the Navy."

"Okay," he said.

"My name is Diane," she said to cheer him up. "Diane Reamer.

"I'm Fred Cole." The merry old sole, he didn't say.

"You will come, won't you?"

They shook hands. He tried to make it tongue-in-cheek, a parody of formal meeting, but in the handshake he felt her little sparrow soul curled up and fluttering in the palm of his hand.

Saturday night, he wandered around the streets of Boston trying to shake off the image of the golden girl on the soda pop ad by patronizing honky-tonks. Girls from Paris called to him. The international coterie of full-color posters and cheap wine smells, all pointing to seduction, dazzled him, and his flesh played havoc with his ideals. He had dreams of Diane running down the subway stairwells with a pajama top flying over her shoulder, ready to model, squinting slightly because she either couldn't see or made believe she couldn't. Heads turned on the platform, in the car. In the studio as well. He took up painting to see her white body, possessing it with brush and oils, incarnating it on canvas. But he would never quite get the shade of white he wanted. To get a whiter white, add drops of black paint, he knew. So he added one black drop, then another; but since it still wasn't white enough to incarnate the whiteness, he added another black drop to the other drops of black.

Sunday he got a brainstorm. If you can't make a girl over in your image, just make her. Preach water, drink wine. He drove over to Harvard Square, wasted half an hour trying to park, then, hoping to surprise her, dragged his feet up the old brown stairs to the third floor. Ascending, his armpits began to drip sweat. It's not anticipation, it's the climb, he said, looking up to the pinnacle of the brown banister, a shining wood globe. Suppose she's not home. He cursed his body for betraying him, for compromising the sense of courage and savoir-faire he had urged into his head. She's got to be home, and alone, he said. He saw her clad in her model's shift. Stopped, breathed, felt the ringing hope down to his loins.

Now that his id had sensed a whiff of coition, haste conquered prudence and raced him, twitching, up the stairs. But where was he rushing to, three steps at a time? Some are born to lick their chops, others only to drool. Some to hatch visions, others to scratch them. The only thing Freddie Cole kin hatch, chanted a ring of girls circling in his skull like a crown of thorns, is a fart. The banister slowly cycled down to him. Oppressed by the strategy of entrance, he touched, grabbed the round wooden head of the old banister as a sanctuary, lungs pumping like shop-worn bellows. His head reeled, dizzy from the brown climb to the top floor. Saw three brown doors. One immediately off the head of the stairs. He sucked deep—exhaled, rather; the john stench seeping from the threshold overwhelmed him, like the two-pronged slap of a sweat-drenched towel: wind preceding matter.

At the other end of the narrow hall were two other doors, at right angles. A paper nametag in the door on the left read: Wally Wickles, PhD. The other door was Diane's. Now for the loud or soft knock. Or the buzzer, blasé or polite. Focused his glance, and saw the door ajar. Cautiously, he stuck his head in. From within, rhythmic and muffled, came the furtive sounds of love. Turn back, he was told. He watched the back of his own figure receding—and hunched over—down the stairs. Blinked and moved his hand over the place where the doorknob should have been. Then he flipped off the switch to his intellect and followed his heart.

He tiptoed in, thinking—after he crossed over and turned right into the hallway—Now or never. His eyes grinding away like a camera in the musty spice-filled air of a Sunday afternoon, he looked down the tiny hall, saw the telephone table to the right, the huge lithograph of Degas dancers above it. Immediately to the left was a small washroom with sink, tub, shower, but no bowl, fluttering under the weight of drying panties and bras. There were baby oils and baby lotions and baby powders all over the place. The place smelled like the inside of a slightly damp compact. Next door, and no bigger, the kitchen, overflowing with a leaning tower of dirty dishes. Stepped out into the hallway again. About seven feet ahead was the wooden partition on which a sign: "Elly's Inn." Behind it, the bed, the source of the moans.

The Degas dancer was leaning out the picture, ready to answer the phone. What if it rang and he were caught here? He cocked an ear, concluded that at the rate Elly and her friend were going, they wouldn't bother to move. He tiptoed forward, past the telephone table to a door on his right. Diane's room, empty. He took one step, froze as he heard a thrashing noise on Elly's bed. Four naked legs crashed out of the left frame of the partition, peeking out as though through a stage curtain.

Fred Cole looked around quickly. To his left, a curtained clothes rack. To his right, Diane's room with its closet of sliding wall-to-ceiling doors. Followed his heart and slipped behind the curtain.

Closer now, he heard them struggle and giggle.

"I'm going to the john," the guy said. "Swipe any good books lately?"

"Oh keep still, Billy. Take that Fielding book."

"How do you manage those fat ones? Don't they ever catch you?"

"Uh-uh. Too clever. But campus patrol almost caught up to me Friday. Luckily the car I hitched with speeded away. A real cops and robbers chase."

Fred moved behind the dresses until he came to a crack in the cloth. Saw a sailor cap on the floor, and the campus patrol on the permascreen of his memory. His skin tingled, from cloth and anger. The "Elly's Inn" sign had been put there to mislead him. It was her voice all right from behind the partition; sad and complaisant, with that dull razor edge, as though the sharpness had been rubbed away.

Diane's legs coiled back into the frame again. She yawned. Cole, peeking, saw half a naked hirsute cheek stepping into a pair of shorts. "Where's the key?" Billy barked.

"On the phone table," Diane said. Billy brushed past. The cloth waves undulated on Cole's face.

"Where the hell is it?" Billy said, banging the phone. "Never mind," Diane said. "The door is open anyway. Wally Wickles, our john partner, doesn't get home 'til late today. Anyway, he's got a pisspot. . . . Now don't you wake me when you get back."

"Screw you. I didn't come here to nap." Screw her is right, Fred thought, seething, watching love and lust exchanging places.

He strained forward to catch a momentary glimpse of Diane's naked back. She pulled the sheet over her head. He watched the sculpted sheet. So that's what she looks like in her art studio. No dou—

When with a curse she threw off the sheet and jumped up. She went, stark naked, breasts swinging, to a chest of drawers—Fred thought his heart would burst at the beauty of it; he hardly knew which button to (sup)press to avoid this. She fumbled around, and as she pulled out one black sleeping mask, another dropped to the floor. She went back to bed, facing the wall.

Fred, ears alive and humming, heard the bathroom door slamming. The son of a bitch, he thought. What right has he got? Just because he's her cousin does he think he can. . . ? He stared at the black mask on the floor. Infuriated, hot, giddy from the dark clandestine air, he was struck with an idea. He slipped out of his hiding position, at once found the bathroom key under the phone, and trotted to the bathroom. Key in hand, he pressed his ear to the door. What's taking him so long? Finally it began. At the height of the stream, Fred Cole swiftly inserted the key and turned the lock, then ran back, key in hand to the apartment door. He locked that door manually and dropped the key into his pocket.

Now the noise began, muted through the locked doors, of fists pounding. He picked up the black mask and donned it, peeking through the tiny slits at Billy's puddle of clothing.

He scanned the room through the mask, could feel the black border on his eyes. The room changed. His heart beat quicker. A pirouette across the room. He drew the window curtain. In the dusk, he unzipped his trousers and worked with all fours to undress. Sailing in the air with the glory, the black magic of it all, he levitated next to Diane. His soda pop madonna. Stripped the sheet back. Diane moaned in her sleep. Even in the semi-darkness her white ass shone like a halo. Adjusting his mask, he leaped—hop, skip, and hump—into the bed and pressed himself to her back. She mumbled, "Let me sleep," but adjusted herself to him. As he embraced her, cupping both breasts with one hand, her soft underbelly with the other, she turned suddenly and screamed: "Aieee. You have one too."

He nodded.

She turned back. "I told you to let me sleep, wretch. Not now . . . What's that banging?"

"Doctor Wickles," he said through clenched teeth, into her neck.

"He locked himself in, the absent-minded professor goof," she laughed, as Fred nuzzled her neck, her shoulders. The banging grew louder. Determined to silence it, Fred Cole continued nuzzling until her protests grew weaker, so weak, killing two birds with one stone now, he could hardly hear her moaning for the pulse beats exploding in his ears.

It was dark now. He got up, dressed, making sure to step into his own puddle of clothes. He pirouetted again, with new life, and ripped off the mask. Pleased with himself, he slapped his hands lightly and strode to the bathroom door. Once in a while a faint knock of protest came from within, followed by a short-lived impassioned barrage.

"Let me out, bitch."

"At once, Mr. Nottingham."

"My name is Bill Wooster, and I'm over the hill. I'm gonna be AWOL."

"Right you are, Mr. Nottingham," Cole said, walking away. He was hungry. The kitchen was a mess. There were dishes dishes everywhere, but not a crumb to eat. The fridge contained a can of tomato sauce, a raw egg, some eggnog mix, beheaded animal cookies, a jar of sour pickle juice, and the cellophane wrapper of some light-diet bread. Heard a girl's laughter coming up the stairs. She shouted to someone. Nottingham-Wooster found renewed vigor and resumed his knocking. Fred ran out, quietly closed the apartment door, and walked to the head of the stairs. Elly was just rounding the bend half a flight down.

"Hi there. Who you? What's all the banging here?"

"Shh." He motioned her forward, out of earshot, toward the apartment. "My name's Fred Cole—"

"Oh yes, so you're the silent one. Diane told me all about . . ."

"Look, I just got here myself a couple of minutes ago and wanted to use the bathroom. Then I heard that insane banging. I got so mixed up listening to this kook over here's raving that I didn't even knock yet. Is Diane home?"

"I don't know." Elly looked down over the banister.

"Sure she's home, the bitch. Lemme out. Lemme out. What is this, Russia?"

"Expecting someone?" Cole asked Elly.

"My boyfriend, Oscar. He went to find a parking place. What's with the kook in the john?"

"Seems your neighbor, Winkles—"

"Wickles—"

"—locked this guy in there," Fred whispered. "Drunk. And he wants him to sober up. He has a crush on Diane."

"Who doesn't?" said Elly. "Never a dull moment in Harvard Square. Where's Wickles?"

"Went out for coffee."

Fred walked back to the john door. He spoke louder now. "This guy's name is Nottingham, but he insists it's Wooster. Watch this. Not, not who's there?"

"Wooster," said the strained voice.

Fred nodded significantly at Elly. "What'd I tell you?"

Elly leaned over the banister, laughing. Fred ran his glance up from her slim ankles to the soft underside of her knees. As if feeling the caress, she kicked up a leg.

Fred stepped up to Elly; he brushed back the hair from her ear and whispered, "Do you think he's dangerous?" just as another fusillade of bangs seemed to bend the old wooden door.

"Now let me out, you sons a bitches. If I get hold of the mother—"

Fred politely cupped his hands over Elly's receptive ears. They were warm ears, attractive ears, fine, smooth-skinned ears. For extra insurance, Elly pressed her hands over his.

"What language!" she said.

Somehow, in the protective interchange, Cole found himself pressed up to her. A monkey cookie with a lecherous grin leered at him. Felt another surge of lust coming on. Elly, ears covered, bent over to watch for her boyfriend.

"Parking is tough around Harvard Square. Once it took him forty minutes. You have trouble parking today?"

"Nope. I've had a streak of luck so far."

She gave him a look that melted his already thawed-out heart. Fred Cole had fallen in love again. Celebrating, he knocked on the john door. "Not, not, who's not there? Is it Nottingham, or not Nottingham, in twenty-five words or less?"

The captive responded by throwing himself full tilt against the door. Fred took hold of Elly.

"Let's get out of here," he told her. "The guy is dangerous."

"How can we? Oscar's parking the car, lover boy. He'll be up here any minute." She put her hands on his face, her fingers trembling against his cheeks. "You know, I once bet Diane five bucks—God, she owes me so much money five won't make any difference—that I could seduce you. But Diane insisted you weren't the type. She said you were silent stolid puritan to the bedrock."

"Want to win your bet?"

"The bet's off," she whispered. "Cause the ground rules have changed."

A door slammed. Someone was whistling, "I Can't Give You Anything but Love, Baby."

"It's Oscar. Sorry, Freddy," she whispered. "Some other time. It's our love-hour now."

"By the way, Diane's in your bed. She doesn't want to be woken up."

"We'll use her room," Elly said automatically, then, "I thought you said you—"

Fred looked down, playing the role, smiling bashfully at his shoes. Before he knew it, Elly had grabbed the back of his head and kissed him on the lips, trotting off to the door. "Tell him I'm in Diane's bed and not to put on the lights."

Oscar spiralled his whistling tune up the stairs.

Fred watched him. Oscar was a slightly built, handsome boy, with broad shoulders, long arrogant eyes, and dark black hair, thick at the sides, like an unemployed actor. When they looked at each other, they saw green flames. It was hate at first sight.

Fred waited until Oscar brushed by him.

"You Oscar?"

Oscar looked him up and down.

Fred retreated metaphysically, about to short-circuit himself off, stare away anyplace than face those mocking cocksure green eyes. Then he remembered; the black mask, Diane, the monkey cookie, Elly's ears. So he looked Oscar up and down.

"Yes," Oscar said.

"Elly told me to tell you—"

"Where is she—and who the hell are you?"

"What's it to you who I am? I have a—"

"Lemme out," Wooster began pounding. "Call the cops, mister. I hear a new voice out there. Hear me out, mister. Please." Oscar took one look at the latrine door, then turned and pushed Cole aside. "What is this, buster, some sort of practical joke?"

Cole charged the apartment door and caught hold of Oscar. The mask, pirouetting with ideas and adventure. The avatar of Fred Cole, metamorphed by a key, a closet, and a black mask.

"You hear that banging, Oscar? Now listen." He pulled out the john key. "See this?" he whispered. "Diane just locked a buddy of her neighbor Wickles in there because he was drunk and made some passes at and some obscene remarks about Elly."

"What?"

"He said Elly had the nicest white ass this side of the Mason-Dixon line."

"I'll kill him. I'll kill the son of a bitch. He said that?"

"In there," Fred Cole nodded toward the john. "Drunk."

"Give me that key. I'll kill him."

"Take it easy." Fred held him back with one hand and with the other dangled the key just out of Oscar's reach.

"The son of a bitch. I'll kill him."

"The guy is stewed, Oscar. No need to fight. He's over it now."

"Gimme. Gimme, I said. Give it to me."

Cole brought the key closer. "See how he just feebly bangs on the door once in a while. So let him out will you?"

"You bet I'll let him out. Just give me that goddamn key."

Fred pressed the key into his hand and spun into the apartment door. He opened it, pirouetted once, bowed to the john, and locked the door to the apartment. Waited, ears pressed to the wood. Fred could not see through the door, no, but what he heard was sweeter than sight. Ears aglow, eyes beatifically pressed shut, he had a vision of the key turning, the door opening, and one hundred-eighty pounds of johnned-up rage blasting into freedom. He heard one punch, knew who crumpled whom with one fist swing. When the victor bent over the vanquished, Fred stepped into Diane's room, closed the door, and by no means made any effort to turn on the light.

"Oscar honey, what took you so long? That goddamn parking, huh? Is that rumpus still going on out there, sweetie? What do you say?"

Fred didn't say, but whistled, "I Can't Give You Anything but Love, Baby," tugging, whistling while he worked, from the upswing of the shirttails to the decrescendo of the zipper. He felt his way along the wooden doors and, for the heck of it, miming conspiracy, danger, what-have-you, walked through to the other end. Dresses, coats, blouses brushed his naked body. He slid open the door and stepped, still whistling, out of the close closet air.

She whistled back.

They heard Diane getting up next door to answer the banging on the door.

"Don't come in, Diane," Elly shouted. "Oscar's in here."

"Who's that banging on the door?" Diane asked. "The son of a bitch Billy left without saying goodbye. That's the Navy for you. Just a minute."

Cole held his breath, and Elly's too, as he heard the door unlocking.

Diane screamed.

"Shit," Wooster burst in. "What the hell is going on? Who's the guy I conked in the hall?"

"Leak," Fred hissed quickly and jumped out of bed. Swept up his clothes and slipped back into the closet. Heard Diane running toward the john. A moment later she shouted, "You killed him. You killed poor Oscar."

Quickly Fred backed in, sidestepped back—home again—into the security, the warmth, the imaginative greenhouse seethe of the closet.

"Oh," Elly catapulted from the bed, "no!" passing Fred, who, through the closet, saw her darkly sailing by. She slid one closet door open and Fred, playing along, slid along. She put on a bathrobe, inside out, and dashed outside. Fred saw it all, through the closet wall: Elly bending over the prostrate Oscar, rushing back wrathfully at Nottingham-Wooster, both girls now lacing into him: Elly into Nottingham, Diane into Wooster.

"Get out you ingrate," Diane shouted, "and put your pants on."

"Poor Oscar," Elly said. "Steps out for a leak and look what the drunken bum does. What'd he do to you?" she asked Wooster.

"Lock me in the goddamn john for an hour."

"He couldn't have," Diane said. "It must have been that absent-minded prof neighbor of ours."

"Don't give me that bluffing crap. It was him, this guy. I don't know him from Adam but you should of seen the way he tore into me soon as I opened the door. Just wait 'til he wakes up. I'll just clobber him back to sleep. Again."

"You will huh?" said Elly and slid the closet door open,

in her frustration speaking to it: "Get me a hanger," unperturbed that it responded like a vending machine. A moment later—a smile lurked in the closet: in triumph, Cole ran in one door, out the other; chasing his shirttail—Cole heard the yelp of pain, wood striking bone, the hanger banging Wooster.

Flirting with getting caught, a way of making safety even more secure, and revving up his daring, Cole kept sliding the doors back and forth, stepping in and out, achieving a rhythm, a dance, viewing the celluloid image of himself, giddy and drunk, divested of gravity, invested with grace. Then, exhausted, Fred moved back to the closet. It was good in there. Hiding, hidden, but like a good puppeteer, managing the strings, heart and G, from behind the curtain. So dark and quiet and comfortable. If no one had ever written a love song to a closet, he would. Eyes closed, he saw Elly bending over Oscar now, holding his head and watching his fluttering eyelids, coaxing him to get up. Inside the apartment Diane was shouting to Wooster to get out.

"Here's the rest of your clothes, now scram, brute. Animal. Swine. And to think I neglected that poor Freddy Cole for you."

"And who the hell is poor Freddy Cole? Just let me lay my hands on him."

"That's all you know. Out, you oaf!"

"And all you know is swiping. Don't think I didn't notice the ten-spot you lifted from my wallet last time I was in."

"You're a goddam liar. You have no character, no style. And me exchanging poor Freddy Cole with a heart of gold for a brawny, hand-swinging fascist peasant . . ."

Here Cole in self-pity wiped a tear away with a silk chemise that had been tickling his ears. He got Diane's hint and it touched him where it hurt the most. He got the hint all right and flexed his running legs—no need for mask at all now—jogging in place, hot to trot and gallop to the goal again.

"Take inventory, Wooster," Diane was saying. "Underwear, pants, suit, sailor cap, anchor. Anything missing? Now get out—"

"I went AWOL for you, ingrate."

"Who asked you to? Go back to the ship and defend us against our worldwide enemies."

"Blood's thicker than water, cousin. Bitch."

"So's wine. But liquor's quicker. Prick."

"Just one kiss to keep peace in the family."

"All right. Piecemeal, kiss my ass."

"Ladies first," he said, dodging the slap, sprinting out, hopping over Oscar, then sliding, spiraling, down the banister.

"How's Oscar, Elly?" Diane asked.

"He's coming around, mumbling about a key. Let me take him to your bed. It's quieter there."

Cole waited, in the closet, until the three were near the bed, the girls fussing with Oscar. Fred stepped out, stood rock still for a moment, savoring the danger—puritan to the bedrock, ha!—looking at the backs of Diane and Elly just long enough to invoke a sense of bravado, and stepped out into the anteroom. He eyed Elly's empty bed; imagined Diane's naked form in it and carefully sketched out all the details. Next move, out of the apartment and into the hall. Breathed deeply, to enroot the sense of change and make it permanent, he set his face with an expression of hope, slight daring, and injured pride. He walked back to the door and knocked.

"Now who can this be?" Diane shouted. "Shit! This place is like Grand Central at Christmas. Is that you again, Wooster?"

"No it's me, Nottingham."

"Who?"

She opened the door.

"Can I come in?" Cole asked shyly.

"Freddy, I was just talking about you. Of course you can. Hey, let me take a look at you. You look pooped."

"I've been working." He gazed at her face, the lines under her eyes working their way through the make-up, unskillfully applied, childish in that unskill, and that alone making her lovable. Searched her helpless baby face, so innocent-looking, so mask-like, so lost. Remembered her moaning, which had nowhere to go but sideways. For the first time he felt sorry for her. At least he could take the mask off when he wanted to.

"You been selling?" she said. "On Sunday?"

"Yup. What with parking and samplers to dish out. I'm—"

She took his hand.

He walked, still holding her hand—but who was leading whom?—to the bed he had seen before. Diane's mask was on the floor; there was a footprint on it. It brought a tear to his eye. Without a word, as though they'd been talking forever, their arms ran ahead of their thoughts. He blanked out and, through the mask on the floor, stepped back into the closet. He touched her hair again. So it wasn't real after all. The sunbeams washed through his fingers, staining them. He clasped Diane, combining the enthusiasm of firsts with the appetite of seconds. He lay still for a while and watched her. That life-dulled look had come over her face again. Unlike a candle, she had passed on a flame, but left no spark for herself. Gently, he turned her face toward him.

She submitted, gazed at—through—him. She blinked, squinted, slow and cold. The darkness of a Sunday evening, the cruelest dusk of the week, ate into him. That goal-less moaning began once more, seeping into him, anesthetizing him, robbing him of joy. He thought of her thumb, beckoning his car, her fingers, her hands.

She gripped his forearms, whispered suddenly, “I owe you three bucks.”

“It’s all right. Don’t worry about it”

“I’ll pay it back,” she said.

He weighed her blonde hair, now browning at the roots. She placed her hand on his back and withdrew, embracing him. Following, he raced along, remitting desert justice, hand for hand, stroke for stroke.

She made a noise. He couldn’t tell if it was pain from the heart or a frustrated cry.

“What is it?” he asked.

“You know, dammit,” she said.

“I’m sorry,” he said.

“I know. Let’s forget it. It’s like waiting for Kingdom Come.”

Dead to each other’s arms and minds, they both made love to ghosts, (un)screwing each other’s ideals.

A GENTLEMAN CALLER; OR, THE ABSOLUTELY LAST AND FINAL FAREWELL APPEARANCE OF AYZIK KLASS

Ayzik Klass, the Yiddish artist, was dead. Gone from the scene at seventy, or sixty-nine, depends which encyclopedia you read. For four days his mourning Griselda told no one. She had him buried privately. There was no eulogy, no minyan, no Kaddish, no funeral.

Still, Klass was not gone from the scene. In fact, he was more in the scene than ever. At home, in Washington Heights, the widowed Griselda had a drizzly feeling of discontent. Every day, during the last three days, from the time of the reluctant announcement of Klass's passing, Griselda Klass (please pronounce it *Klaaahss*, the British way) got a little packet. Once an envelope. Once a little box. Once a book bag. And in each, wrapped in a tissue, was a little white plastic hospital spoon with its head neatly snapped.

It's revenge, she thought. He's getting even.

Seven days after Ayzik Klass's death, when the unobserved

shiva period should have been over, the phone rang in Griselda's apartment. It was 9:58 p.m.

"Hello," she said weakly. She wanted everyone to know how mournful she was, that even her greeting was pregnant with dolor.

"Hello," came the response. A pause then a tentative "Hello" again. "I'm coming back."

"What?" she screamed into the phone.

"I'm coming back," Ayzik Klass repeated in his Polish-Yiddish accent, and the phone went dead.

All of a sudden Griselda had a vision, like a film seen twice. Saw again how she had told no one. Ordered the doctors and the hospital not to tell the newspapers. It was her absolute right. How she invited two women to her apartment in Washington Heights, the .75 friends she had, served them tea and two dry biscuits and chatted amicably. How she said, "Let's not discuss it now," when they asked how Klass was feeling. How she then called a limousine service from another room, waited outside with them, and as the black car pulled up, said gravely, grandly, "We're going to a funeral."

"Whose?" they wanted to know.

"Klass's."

He called to drive her mad, she knew. His punishment. Revenge. He vowed he'd get even with her for not taking him to the hospital in time. Even there he shouted with his last fistful of strength, purposely, to humiliate her. "Why you on purpose waited three hours to call the ambulance, hah? Why you waited so long when I beg you to give me the phone, you anti-Semitt? Why you kept saying it is indigestion?" She told the doctors he was delirious; the medications were making him insane. But he didn't stop. He ranted on. "Why you wait to call the airconditioning man? Why you always put cakes and herring and fatty foods in front of me when I'm overweight, hah?" Now he stopped for a breath. Shut his eyes. Opened them and said, "And most, why you told me you're not—" And in horror she clapped a hand over her mouth and he stopped. At least he didn't make *that* public.

Griselda, hand still on the receiver, as if sentenced to hold it, sat like a stone. Klass's words rang dully in her ears. My God! He called. He's dead. He's going to kill me. Snap my head like one of those plastic spoons. Her hand leaped from the phone as if it were a live wire, or a corpse. Then she let out a shriek. She bared her teeth, raised her head, clawed the air and shrieked, caught her breath, shrieked again. Did not know she was capable of such unearthly cries. She ran to the door, thought of running into the hall and screaming there, to get some comfort. Then realized that her neighbors on the floor, whom she hadn't even told, would not likely give her comfort. She ran back to the living room and screamed into the sofa pillow. How would she ever leave the apartment if he stood there, waiting at the door? Klass had planned it then, to get back at me after his death. That's why he didn't let me die first. So he could come back and haunt me. Drive me mad. But he's *not* going to drive me mad. I'd rather die.

She went to the window. No, he wasn't going to drive her to jump eighteen floors. She caught her contorted face in the mirror as she ran through the apartment and put on all the lights. Didn't know why she ran. Just wished to get away from where she was. She'd always been afraid of intruders, but now—worse, worse—there was an intruder from within.

She ran to the kitchen, opened the refrigerator, Klass's half-finished schmaltz herring still there, the sign WATCH WHAT YOU EAT still there, and returned to the phone. It was ten-thirteen.

She checked the door. Double-locked. Why didn't he call after eleven when the rates were cheaper? She wanted to take the phone off the hook, but he could call even that way. And if the phone rang with the receiver off the hook she would die. She picked up the phone, said "Hello" slowly, heart beating, half expecting an answer. She jumped into bed with all her clothes on, did not—as she usually did—look in the closet or under the bed. Fell asleep that way.

The next morning, the flood rush of memory vised her heart. She told no one. Who would believe her? Oh God, oh God, why did I do it? Why didn't I tell him who I was when we met? Why did I tell him that awful day and make him ill? Why did I want to get even with him *that* way? Now he's . . . and she pressed her fist into her mouth and felt herself going white. He's going to kill me. She felt the blood running from her head. As if someone were sucking the breath from her. Still, beneath the fear, a pleasant hope. Perhaps he would come back and she would make it up to him, devote her life selflessly to him, baby him, argue with him no longer. Eat as much as you want. If you have another attack, at once to the hospital. Read as much as you like. Paint not at all. Go to galleries. Stain not one of your fingers with dirty paint. And when, *if*, you die again, I'll make you such a funeral, everyone will be invited. And it will be a catered affair.

That day she didn't leave the house, afraid to open the door. That night she had two calls. Each one made her heart stop, but they were from the other secretaries she knew at her school, asking how she was.

At ten o'clock she looked at the clock and waited. Eleven came and went. She breathed easier. Maybe that was the end of it. She waited half an hour and then, feeling a weariness filling her body like heavy syrup in a bottle, lay down to sleep.

At midnight the ringing jolted her like an electric shock.

"Hello?"

"Hello. I'm coming back," Klass said. "I'm coming back."

"Leave me alone," she screamed. "Stay where you are. Don't torture me."

He chuckled. "I'll call you same time tomorrow."

This time she did not scream. She tried, but no sounds came.

"It's a bad dream," She said aloud. "I . . . will . . . go . . . back . . . to . . . sleep. Do you hear me?" she warned herself. "I will go back to sleep."

She slept fitfully; horrible dreams. In one, Klass stood at the door alive and well; in another, he was dead, in his shroud, pale and gaunt, his white hair in disarray, his black eyebrows starker than ever. After a polite knock, he walked in through the unopened door, and calmly announced, "Now we'll make arrangements for the funeral the proper way, the Jewish way. First we'll call the Yiddish papers. Then the art journals. Station WEVD. Here's a list of my friends. I want it done to me like it was done to my father's father and his fathers before him. A living funeral. Not a dead one. Not with hysteria, egoism, or lies."

In the middle of the night she woke. Could not sleep any more. With whom could she discuss this? Her few friends wouldn't believe her. It would have to be someone outside her circle. Someone less intimate. Someone who wouldn't consider her mad. She spun an imaginary dial in her mind and the number stopped at Professor Norwald Winters Robinson, the man who had written the best seller on the Holocaust. She'd been at his NYU office months ago, showing him some of her husband's slides. The big man had made vague promises. Seemed to be more interested in her, that lecher, than in Klass's oil paintings. But he did come to Klass's show.

She called information but he had an unlisted number. Then she looked and found it in Klass's directory on his little desk.

Jarred, startled, he grunted, "Hello?"

"Hello, this is Griselda."

"Who?"

"Griselda Klass."

"Do you know what time it is?"

"Oh. Just a minute. I'll go to the kitchen. My clock here is unplugged."

She dropped the receiver; it clacked against the side of the night table in decreasing little beats like a metronome gone awry. Robinson's head cleared. He imagined telling his friends, "That idiot, she wakes me at 3 a.m. and I tell her, 'Do you know what time it is?' and that whacky loon runs to the kitchen and tells me . . ."

"It's three-oh-three. You see, the clock face next to my bed is lit up and I can't stand the evil green winking at me when I try to sleep so I unplug it."

"But when you sleep how can you see it?"

"What if I wake up?"

"Then you're not asleep anymore."

She didn't say a word.

"Any other reason you called besides to tell me the time?" Robinson asked.

Again a pause.

"I called you? You called *me*! Wait a minute. You're right. I'm sorry. I'm so mixed up. You'll understand why when I tell you. Something strange has happened."

Now Robinson sat up. He swung his hulk from a rather uncomfortable half-reclining position to a normal one, with his legs on the floor. He shook his head. Nothing cleared. The conversation was as absurd as ever. He remembered when she had shown him her husband's slides, she pressed her breasts into his arm as he held the slides up to view. Biggest bazooms he'd ever seen. She's a widow, he repeated to himself. She's confused. Excuse her behavior. Civility demands it.

"I'm listening, Mrs. Klass."

"Griselda. Please call me Griselda."

"I read about the terrible news. I'm so sorry. Such a talented man. Didn't know how to reach you. Unlisted number . . . A loss for us all . . . Can I help you in any way?"

"Yes, please. I need your help. Something awful happened, and that's why I called in the middle of the night."

"Don't cry. What's the matter?"

"I got two terrible calls the last two nights . . ."

"Crank calls?"

"No. Worse."

"Have you called the police?"

"No. No. Police can do nothing in a case like this. It's terrible . . . creepy . . . Mr. Robinson . . . would you . . . dear Professor . . . I hate to impose, but I think . . . we have to talk in person."

"Sure. Fine. Where can we meet? In my office?"

"No. Impossible for me to leave the house." Then she said it all at once. "Would you come here and I'll tell you more?"

"When should I come?"

She wanted to say now, but then he would refuse and she wouldn't be able to ask him again.

After Robinson had identified himself behind the closed door, assured her he was alone and no one—nothing—stood next to him, Griselda opened the door, quickly whisked the tall man in, and told him everything.

"Incredible," he said, expressing amazement at the story and even more at the small apartment. He assumed all artists were rich men. “And you told no one?”

“I was afraid they’d laugh at me. You I trust.”

Griselda’s fingers stretched out toward Robinson, as if soon they would clutch his shoulders for protection. The big prof had a healthy imagination. Also, for a bachelor he was a very erotic man. He watched her fingers, looked at her face. Hardly made up; a light dusting of powder that made her pale face paler. She must be years younger than Klass. Mid-forties, probably, but in excellent shape. That body. That seductive form. Blonde hair, dyed no doubt, scared, vulnerable, looking for support, the fingers dying to leap from trembling against her chin to his shoulders.

“What time did he say he would call?” Robinson said quickly to show her *he* didn’t think she was mad. He looked serious.

“He said he’ll call back at the same time. But he called an hour later, after eleven o’clock. The rates are cheaper.”

Robinson swallowed. He wasn’t going to laugh. He quickly looked up, saw what he saw.

“Oh,” Robinson marvelled. “A Chagall! Of Klass!”

“Yes, of course. Good friends. Great friends. They painted each other in Paris in 1946. Another reason I told no one was that it would have leaked out to the press, and I wanted to spare that dear old man the trouble of flying to the funeral of my most beloved husband. I’m sure Marc won’t forgive me, for he would have come. I’m going to write him a letter of apology.”

“Do you want me to stay ’til the call comes?”

“If midnight is too late for you, I’ll understand. But yes, please, stay. I’ll pay for your taxi home. You can get on the extension and listen just to convince me I’m not going mad. I want you to believe me, Mr. Robinson.”

"Don't call me Mr. Robinson. Call me Norwald."

"You must hear for yourself. Don't just take my word. You've spoken to him. You know his voice."

"Sure, I know his voice. We met at the opening of his show. About five-six months ago?" Robinson shook his head, remembering. "And I'll stay 'til after the call. No one you know imitates him, doing some kind of trick?"

"Who could, who would, do a nasty thing like that? So few know our phone number. And anyone can see through an imitation."

At midnight the phone rang. "Pick it up. Pick it up." she yelled hysterically. "In my bedroom. I'll answer here. Listen carefully. You remember his voice?"

"Yes, yes. Answer it," said Robinson.

She picked up the phone.

"Hello?"

"No use to lock the door," Klass said. "Locks don't affect me anymore."

"Get away from me. By all that's holy, get away from me," she screamed. "Don't call any more. Don't. Please!"

Robinson covered the receiver and yelled from the bedroom, "Ask him to say something that's unique to him."

"If it's really you, Klass, tell me, prove to me it's you."

"The purpose of my art is to revivify the dead."

Griselda's head fell back against the wall.

"Don't call again. I believe you. What are you doing to me? All my life I devoted myself to you. For your sake I didn't have children. Have pity. Don't call again." She felt herself sliding down the wall to a sitting position. "Please. Don't. Call. Again. PLEASE. Go back. You're dead."

"I want a second opinion," Klass said.

* * *

She hung up and began to scream, first a meld of laughter, hysterical and choking yelps, then one long piercing wail. Robinson ran in and lifted her. On her feet, she stumbled with him to the bedroom and sank into the bed.

Robinson sat tentatively on the edge, like on a bathtub.

"Did you hear? You heard him. It's him, right?"

"Him. No doubt."

Robinson's nostrils flared. He pressed his lips, suppressed the rising laughter. Second opinion! He bit his lips until they hurt.

"That phrase . . . It sums up all his ideas: the purpose of my art is to revivify the dead . . ." She gave a start. Her head sunk to her chest. The blonde hair, in disarray, covered her face. "My God! Now I understand. All his work was a rehearsal for this. To come back and haunt me . . . What's that noise? Did you hear that? Is that him at the door?"

"He didn't say he's coming back, though." Robinson noticed the quaver in his own voice. "Did you notice that?"

"Yes. But who knows? Can the dead be trusted?"

A knocking at the door.

Griselda stood, began trembling. Then, suddenly, she pressed her head to his chest, arms around Robinson's back.

Scared himself, he hugged her too.

"Someone knocking." Robinson's voice sounded dead. His knees shook. There was a funny feeling in his bladder. Would he lose all control?

The knocking again. Three taps. Pause. Three taps again.

"Is that his knock?"

"God, what should I do?"

"Go ask who it is." His voice tried to be firm and authoritative. But the words came out in a near tremor. He coughed to drive off the affliction.

"You go," she said.

"Me? Me saying 'Who is it?' in my man's voice would be very impolitic," he whispered.

Again the knocking. The pressure awful in his bladder.

"Where's your bathroom?"

"There, through the door. To your right. What if it's him? I'll die. I'm dizzy, dying already. I can't take it. He's killing me, that heartless man. Seven, eight days alone and he can't live without me. Who's making him fried eggs up, or down, there? He's pulling me toward him. I can feel it."

Again the knocking.

Robinson came back.

"Why is he punishing me like that? I know. Because I didn't tell him I wasn't Jewish."

"You? You, the wife of the most famous Yiddish painter in America, not a Jew?"

"No. I'm Ukrainian. A goy like you."

"And he didn't know?"

"He made believe he didn't know. But he knew."

"Who told him?"

"I don't know. Probably one of his many enemies."

The knocking again.

"Well, actually I did," Griselda said. "In the hospital . . . when he was feeling better," she added quickly. "I had to tell him the truth."

"And didn't that shock him . . . I mean, after all, he had a heart attack."

"Oh, no! The medications killed him. There's that knocking again."

She walked to the door on tiptoe, heart rocking.

"Who is it?" she said faintly.

"Open up," said a voice.

"No. NO. NO. I'm not opening the door."

"Open up. It's me. Rivka Berkowitz. Your neighbor from 18F. I heard you screaming. Are you all right? Should I call the police? Or 911? Are you in a hostage situation?"

"No, no, no. Don't interfere. Don't call the police. Who asked you? I'm all right now."

"Ahh . . . I see. I see," Rivka chanted. "I get it. It wasn't screams of pain, but screams of . . . Aha! *Now* I get it!"'

"You get nothing. Get those filthy thoughts out of your head."

"Why are you so angry? When people scream, there's trouble. I want to help you. Don't you want me to come in?"

Griselda leaned her weight against the door. "No, no thank you," she said into the door. She cast a glance back at Robinson, who was waving his hands at her. "I'm all right. Go back to your apartment. Good night!"

She walked back to the bedroom with him.

"Who was it?" Robinson whispered, teeth chattering.

"A neighbor. Heard me screaming. Call police, she said. That's all I need. Look, my hands are shaking."

She nestled into Robinson's protective embrace; both trembled against each other. He felt her hard nipples against his chest.

"Do you think he'll call again?" he asked.

"He only calls once a day. . . . But I'm terrified. . . . What should I do now, Mr. Robinson?"

"Please, Griselda, I told you to call me Norwald."

She pressed her head into his chest, arms limp at her sides. He took out a handkerchief from his jacket pocket and dried her eyes. The gesture made her cry even more. He held her close, thinking: I love the press of her firm flesh.

"I'll protect you from the . . ." Yes, he decided to say it. "From the fierce demon of your husband. No matter what. No matter who calls. Fear not. There is nothing to fear. The only thing we have to fear is fear itself."

Griselda looked up at him. He spoke so beautifully. Yes, this big unselfish man would protect her. He would arrange lectures and she would go around the country and spread the name of her dear late husband. And she would become even more famous. "You're so kind." She kissed her fingertips and touched his cheeks. "Staying with me at a time like this."

Gently, he stroked her forehead and cheeks, her arms and shoulders. Sensing that she was still snuggled to him, he ran his hands down her back, her waist, and up to her breasts, which, ah, finally, unbelievable, he stroked in gradually increasing circular motions. But his fingers got caught in the metal, the ribbing, the paraphernalia of the extensive support system.

"Oh . . . oh . . . oh . . . You have no morals. You are a bad . . . a very bad boy. It's so warm in here. One could die. Oh, you're so good coming to me from so far away."

She lifted her sweater and after several moments of complicated maneuvers behind her back she finally freed the poor incarcerated things. There. That's what he'd been dreaming of for months.

"You realize of course, now that he's gone, I can tell it to the world. He didn't even do a single one of the paintings."

"Really? Incredible! Then who did?"

"Modesty doesn't permit me to say, but I can tell you one thing: How Klass loved my breasts!" she said softly, eyes closed. "He could spend a whole day here. Not even lift a finger. Not paint. Not eat. Imagine! Not even eat. That's how much he loved them. When I first modeled for him in Russia, he said he had never painted such big breasts."

Norwald Winters Robinson swallowed. Should he affirm that indeed they were large and pendulous and the big red nipples strikingly delectable? He was about to say something, but his voice choked. Blue mist swam before his eyes; a thick fog gagged his voice. He didn't know what he was saying.

"What color?"

"I don't remember. But I loved the touch of that soft camel's hair on my nipples, especially when the brush was still new and soft." Slowly she raised her hands. Her breasts responded, lifting up. "How come you never married?"

"Too breasty. Too busy. Too late."

"It's never too late."

"Who wants a fifty-nine, that is, a 50.9-year-old-man?" he said, hoping she would exult, "Me!"

"I would have given everything to have a baby of my own." She rocked her hands. "And have him suckle at my breasts."

Now, he thought. Now. He lunged. Buried his mouth on one breast and kissed it, ran his lips hungrily over it.

She lifted his head away. "No, not that one. You can play with *this* one. The one over the heart was his favorite. It's larger, he said, but then only an artist has an eye for that."

She moved his urging body to the edge of the bed. They stretched out, Griselda on the inside and big Robinson on the rim. He shifted on the sheet.

"I'm falling off."

"I have to leave room," she said. "Suppose he comes back and finds his place taken?"

For a moment Robinson's head spun. He couldn't respond. If absurd has its own logic, he had to say: "First you're scared and now you make room?"

"It's *because* I'm frightened. What will he say?"

"Then what will he say if he finds you in his, my, bed . . . I mean me, us, in your, his, bed."

"You're the man. You think of something."

"I'll think of something." But Robinson lied. He was thinking of nothing, could not possibly think of anything. His head was totally empty. He reached for her breast again. As he touched it, had it almost firmly in his grip, tried to hold it with both his hands, she slipped away like a mermaid in water and jumped up.

"What's the matter?"

"I'm taking the phone off the hook."

He heard her bare feet in the dark, the steps receding, then coming closer. He hoped it was she. If it was Klass he would scream. No shame. Robinson would scream a manly scream, then parachute out the window with a sheet. I'm sleeping here tonight, he wanted to say, firmly in command. Instead, he heard himself saying, "It's too late to go home."

"Don't worry." she said. "You'll sleep here with me. But just sleeping. I'm a recent widow, freshly made, remember?"

"Of course."

"You can understand my concern, my wanting to remember him?"

"Of course. A very commendable approach."

"Klass was a very sexual man. Like he loved food, he loved to love me. He could spend all day not painting, doing you know what. And I didn't mind either. I just read that a woman is most sexual at thirty. That's a lot of salami. Because I kept going. Stronger and stronger. Even Klass at over sixty. Like a centaur. And I, strong and warm at thirty-five, thirty-eight, forty-eight," then quickly shifting gears, "thirty-eight."

"What's that?"

"I said, thirty-eight."

"I thought you said thirty-eight, but in some faint echo, I thought I heard forty-eight."

"Perhaps you thought you heard forty-eight because I said thirty-four."

"Ah, that's it, that's why I must have heard thirty-eight."

"Do you think I'm sick loving it so much?" Griselda asked.

"That's one disease no one wants to cure himself of."

"No, we won't sleep in the middle of the bed. We'll lie on my side. For safety's sake. His part of the bed is reserved for him. Out of respect for the dead. You can hold me so as not to fall off, but remember what you have to remember. I'm a widow. But you can take off your jacket and tie."

"How long will I have to . . . remember?"

"Maybe next week. Or next month. Until I . . ."

The bed seemed to float up as the big man rose.

"Where are you going?"

"Home." he ventured. "I can't take this. What do you think I am, a fourteen-year-old? I'm a grown man. I'm sorry. Good night."

And in the dark he firmly trod toward the door.

"No," she screamed. "Don't go. Don't leave me alone with him." She jumped up and hugged him. Ran his hand over her breasts and belly. "All right," she said gaily, "come here, you dirty man. Shame on you, all six-foot-six-of you." She laughed lightly. "You have no morals, do you? No scruples. No shame. Taking your will on a poor, freshly made young widow. No Christian ethics. No loyalty."

Then slipped out of his grasp again.

"Wait. Where are you going now?" he asked.

"To check the door."

He heard her bare feet tiptoeing in the dark. She banged into things and cursed.

He stood, waiting for her.

She groped in the dark. Something thump-thumped alongside her. She bumped into Robinson.

"I didn't know you used a cane," Griselda said.

"That's not a cane."

"Ow!" Now Robinson bumped into something. "What's that?"

"My husband's picture."

"You took the Chagall down from the wall?"

"In case he comes."

"You're crazy."

"Well, suppose he does come," she whined.

In the dark Robinson couldn't tell if her voice was belligerent or just apologetic. He sat down on the bed.

"Put yourself in my place," she continued. "I'll just lay it between us in the bed and then Klass will know you're here just to protect me, and he should see everything is all right."

Now Robinson jumped up, amazed at his own agility.

"No such thing. You'll destroy this precious painting. You're being absurd. We must be rational. The best I can suggest is that we stand it face to the wall so he can't watch."

They lay down. On her side of the bed. He tried to push further away from the edge.

"That's Klass's side, remember?"

"So it's a *menage a trois*."

"I don't understand Yiddish," she said.

"So there's three of us, huh?"

"Maybe."

"Then I have a problem."

"What?"

"There's really four."

"How? Two and one is three."

"There's two in my party too."

"Who?"

Robinson figured with a kook like Griselda, a demonstrative would go over bigger than a noun. "This!"

"AIEEE!" she yelped, truly amazed. And made room for both of them.

Griselda lay there, on her back, arms stretched out, relaxed, drained. What she had just experienced, like what she had just seen, she had never seen, never thought of in her wildest, most erotic dreams. She had always had big eyes, big desires, little nerve, mortally afraid of her husband's rage, even though he wasn't ashamed to run after other women. Oh, so many shocks had she lately had, and now along comes this. There was a Ukrainian word for it, but she couldn't think of it. True, it was a shock, but it was, how shall she put it, pleasing, pleasant, full of pleasure. It sent a warm little shiver through her. Up it went, swiftly, like those tiny jack-in-the-box pop-ups she'd seen after the war in the Tashkent bazaar. Zhoop! Up went that curl of smoky heat from her loins to her chest and fanned to her shoulders. She even tasted a hot bit of spicy desire in the back of her mouth. The blood thrummed in her ears like a telegraph wire, and she thought of her late husband, God rest his soul and keep him far away from her for now and evermore, voice and all, Amen.

How did the story about Ayzik Klass's calls make the rounds? Griselda confided in no one. The neighbors thought Griselda mad. Robinson kept mum. Still, the story made the rounds; it added fuel to the fiery gossip about Griselda. Though no one believed her, they said she got what she deserved. When Robinson broke his silence after a long while, people doubted him too. After all, why believe Robinson? He always did have a fascination with the dead. Nevertheless, there were rationalists who said it may have been one of Klass's women pals who hated Griselda. Perhaps a female poet who tape-recorded him reading some of her "poems." According to one investigator, the poem might have gone something like this:

I'm coming back, I'm coming back
I'll call same time tomorrow.
No use to lock the door.
Locks don't affect me anymore.

But when the investigator was asked how could one explain the double hello and Klass's ideological summing up, he replied it was simple. Klass said hello twice, tentatively, testing the use of the tape recorder for the first time. And at some other time, the poet had asked the artist for a one-sentence summing up. Perhaps she had planned this as a revenge against her rival. Or perhaps Klass had preplanned the whole affair, getting back at Griselda for the misery she had caused him. Others speculated that with tape, all kinds of miracles can be arranged, not excluding resurrection. And the last perhaps: perhaps the poem part was authentically preplanned, but Klass *did* come back to say hello twice and with a posthumous burst of energy did recall his artistic credo.

The same line of reasoning held for Klass's second-opinion remark. A man who hardly laughed during his lifetime could be permitted one joke, even if it came a little late. And anyway, averred the experts on postmortem telecommunication, everyone was entitled to his opinion, even a dead man.

And others say they wouldn't put it past Ayzik Klass, that artist extraordinaire, to pull off the ultimate stunt, clutching at three dimes and three plastic spoons sewn into his shroud by a willing accomplice and returning for a few moments of revenge to give back to Griselda from the other world a taste of the hell she had for years served up to him in this one.

FINISH THIS STORY

"Finish this story for me, sweetie," Amy said, hands on his face, as she lay next to him and playfully kissed him on the nose. "I must know the ending."

"There's no ending without beginning and middle. You learned that. Aristotle and all that. So why don't you start?"

Okay (she said). Shut the radio. I want you to concentrate on me, not the Top Ten. Thanks. About six months ago, a girl I know, let's call her Rebecca Cohen, who is twenty-eight but looks like a college kid, pretty, chesty—she was once chosen Miss White Plains, you know—brown hair she dyes chestnut, slim waist, slightly assy, sassy, and classy, about five-foot-five in flats, had decided to return to school in order to tie up the loose ends of her life.

"Cliché!" Isaac shouted.

"I know. But sometimes clichés are useful."

"And that assy, sassy, classy rhyme is mine . . . from one of my plays. And furthermore, ladies and gents, note that she returns to school to tie loose ends, like the edges of daddy's long shirt she's wearing, and not, God forbid, to expand

her limited cultural horizons. Limited for her is a clothing store."

Anyway, Mister Sarcastic, she returned to school because she regretted not going to college and was now bored with her life. Since her marriage of five years was—watch two clichés coming—to put it mildly, less than perfect, she now had a new venture, a "baby" she could invest every ounce of her time and energy in: her first semester in Brandeis University.

As Rebecca reviewed her life, certain realities—so she confided in me—her marriage and her relationship to her parents began to surface and she became deeply troubled. There were times her throat was so tight she had difficulty swallowing. She wanted desperately to be a "good Jew" but she wasn't conducting her life as one. She knew that Judaism teaches one to honor father and mother; but because of years of emotional neglect and abuse by a disturbed mother and a weak father she couldn't obey this precept. She hadn't seen her mentally unbalanced mother in years. And more—worse!—she had married a goy, which she knew was the worst thing a Jew could do.

So Rebecca went to school, part-time of course, because she did have a part-time job as a salesgirl in a woman's shop in Boston. Since she hadn't had sufficient exposure in the humanities, she took one course in medieval history and one called Playwriting for Beginners. She figured that if she had to suffer through an obligatory writing course it might as well be drama, which she always liked. For she always had thought of her life as one long drama. Where else but onstage could one have a mother like hers?

"Although she hadn't gone to a play in years. If ever . . ."

"But I was prepared to, remember, Isaac? It's just that the inviter never acted on his promise, as usual."

* * *

The history course was taught by a nondescript young woman, a graduate student who constantly looked at her notes. The writing instructor, Isaac Gelber, was a fairly well-known young American playwright from the University of Iowa Writing Program who was a visiting writer-in-residence here in Brandeis for a year. She was surprised he was so young, just a few years older than her. She expected college profs to be old and mature.

"He was surprised she was so old. He thought she was nineteen."

Rebecca knew he taught two courses. One was an advanced playwriting course for seniors and the other was her beginners course. She looked everything up. She found out he was born in New York, had lived on the West Coast and in the Midwest most of his life, and had written plays about the conflicts of middle-class Jews blending into gentile society. When counselors at the pre-registration seminar for incoming adult students spoke about him, she became curious. By the fourth class session with him, her curiosity became an attraction. It wasn't even an intellectual pull. Yes, she read his plays and even wrote to a New York TV station for a copy of one of his dramas. But it wasn't so much his mastery of the material—that she expected. It was the way he held himself; the confident way he moved; his direct gaze into the eyes of every student; the way he floated, sailed into the classroom.

"Really?" he said. "Actually sailed in?"
"Shh, don't interrupt."

She loved his black curly hair; the sound of his voice. She

even loved the baritone resonance of his "Umm . . ." when he thought about a question. Her attraction wasn't necessarily physical, but nevertheless there was a frisson—

"You stole that word," Isaac said. "Again from me."

—frisson of chemistry, a stirring inside, a warm flush that recalled those pleasant high school crushes. But it must also be said she was jealous that someone just a few years older than her was already famous.

Rebecca is reticent by nature, shy and withdrawn. She would not normally share her thoughts or problems with anyone. But in me she confided. I'm the only one she would speak to. And her professor observed this trait of hers too. In fact, during a conference in his office, he noted that even the way she held her head when she began to talk had a self-effacing quality. Rebecca told me she would think of things to ask her professor after class, just so she could stay and talk with him. About suspension of disbelief, which was new to her. About Aristotle's *Poetics*, brand new. About staging.

She loved talking to him and studying his face. During the first three weeks of class he had a beard. Then, inexplicably, he shaved it off. He now looked boyish, paler, years younger. With the beard gone the dimple of his chin became visible. His lips were now more prominent. As days passed, she loved more and more looking at his face, loved looking into those green eyes, eyes that changed their hue with the weather and with the clothes he wore. She imagined him—was it a daydream?—looking intently at her in class, especially after she had begun talking to him. Could it really be, or was it only Rebecca's powerful dream-wish?

Now she began asking him questions about his own work,

which surprised him, for he didn't make his plays required reading. She asked him if he thought of a face when he created a character and how he felt when an actor filled the role he imagined. She asked him how he arrived at his hilarious definition of democracy in *Movers, Shakers, and Bakers*. He looked at her quizzically, as if he'd forgotten. Maybe he *had* forgotten. You know, she said, where in the play one guy says the difference between democracy and dictatorship is that in a dictatorship you grab *who* you can while in a democracy you grab *what* you can. He laughed shyly and shrugged. And that Jewish woman acrobat in *Flying Hi*, she asked him, was she real or did he make her up? Are there really Jewish acrobats? He answered that after he had written that play a reader wrote mentioning a circus tumbler in ancient Palestine who had become a Talmudic sage, fifteen hundred years ago. And then he told her about a Sarah Mendez, a Sephardic Jew from Holland, one of the famous nineteenth-century acrobats, who worked without a net. And in his two-act TV drama, *San Francisco Seder*, is he hinting at a West Coast Elijah? she wanted to know.

Hey, how did you find all my work? Isaac asked, pleased. She wanted to know more and more, but upon reflection she realized she didn't know what she wanted or what she was doing. What if he suddenly asked her, Why are you asking all these questions? She wouldn't know what to say. His remark would be a needle in her balloon, and she would deflate with a sad pop. What she did know was that it felt so delicious to be beside him talking to him and melting into those green eyes of his. He was gorgeous, she decided. Simply gorgeous. She loved the Monday and Wednesday classes with him because then only one empty day would pass before she saw him again. But her Friday class with him was awful. Because of the intervening weekend the days to Monday dragged by like the Thirty Years War.

She remembers—

"Hey, are you listening?" Amy asked.

"Why do you ask?"

"Because your eyes are closed."

"I'm concentrating. Continue the story."

She remembers the first time he asked her, about six weeks into the semester, if she would like to sit and chat for a while after class. Sure, she said at once. How about next Monday after class? he said. Can't, she said. I have a history tutorial on Mondays and then I'm off to work. Then how about next Wednesday? he suggested. Wednesday's fine. Then she brightened. But today's a Wednesday too. Why not today? she said. Of course! I forgot, he said. Why *next* Wednesday, if today's Wednesday! He sounded so happy. As if he discovered a sudden gift, an extra day in the week. So let's make it today, he said. After next period. Oh, heavens, Rebecca remembers thinking. What did I do? What have I done? She couldn't believe she was so bold. She felt confusion. Ambivalence. I'm married. He's a man. I'm attracted to him. Oh, no! I can't—but I want to.

For the entire next period she couldn't concentrate on the history of the Middle Ages. She mixed up crusades with croissants. Under the guise of a knightly pageant, the previous period's conversation paraded before her eyes. She went over the entire scenario, saw it playacted somewhere behind her eyes, starring him and her. For a moment the Middle Ages interrupted. Then it hit her. The invitation. Why not today? Today's Wednesday too, as if she wanted to be near him. What would he think of her? she wondered. Lately, she had begun taking special care in choosing what she wore to class. She didn't want to look frumpy; she wanted to look pert, bright, pretty, but not overly sexy. Perhaps pretty in a modest way. In the morning she put on and tore off a dozen outfits.

"A dozen?"

"Well, maybe three or four. Sometimes even five."

She rose a half hour earlier to dress—for him. Whereas at the beginning of the semester she might have worn a skirt just a bit too short or a sweater a tad too tight, now she dressed ladylike, as though going to a party or out on a date—with him. Rebecca looked at herself through his eyes. His beautiful green eyes. She read through his plays to see what clothes he gave his heroines. But she was stumped. It wasn't one of his concerns. He was more concerned with what they thought and said than what they wore. His *San Francisco Seder* gave not a clue as to what the women should wear. With no guide to his preference in clothing, Rebecca was on her own. She chose colors and combinations, even textures, that she thought would please him, even tried to translate the timbre of his voice into colors and textures. She knew she had a great figure and wore clothes that showed off her nice breasts and tiny waist. Her tummy was as flat as a ten-year-old's.

"And so was her brain."

Next she worked on her hair, arranging her chestnut waves so as to bring out the deep green of her eyes, the green that so complemented the sparkling tiger green of his.

What indeed would Isaac think of her when they would, as he put it, chat with no other students around? She knew she was ill at ease, disturbed about something. Would he know? After all, this wasn't a student-teacher conference. Was she disturbed because she felt that pull toward him, or did it really have to do with guilt feelings? Guilt feelings freshly minted. For she had once promised herself she'd never break her marriage vows—even though her marriage was shaky and she and her husband had separated two (or was it three?) times.

"Is this making any sense?"

"Of course!"

"Then open your eyes, Isaac."

"I told you I'm concentrating. I close my eyes when I concentrate."

"You're closing your eyes because you're going to use this. Make a play of it. I know. All this is just a playwright's lab for you."

"I won't use your story in a play."

They met in front of the classroom and he said the classroom was no place to talk. Let's take a ride up to the Lookout, he said. Along the way she was too scared to talk. He kept up an inane chatter about pedestrians and bicyclists that had an erratic rhythm and poetry all its own until they parked and strolled into Lookout Park, in the delicious fresh air. They sat opposite each other, cross-legged, on a flat boulder with a view of Waltham down below. A few minutes later, he rose and they began to walk. He said they should do this again. The old story. One always wants more. Little by little, she began to tell him secrets that she had revealed to no one but her husband and that only after several years of marriage. And this prompted a hastened psychological intimacy. Or was it their pristine—

"Hey, come off it, another word that's not yours. Where'd you get that word?"

> *"From the second act of* San Francisco Seder.*"*
> *"Really? Do I use it there?"*
> *"Uh-huh. You see, at least I'm learning."*

—pristine psychological intimacy that prompted her to reveal all with such ease? In other words, did that instinct, that wavelength, that sense of destiny she felt with him prompt her to open up and reveal herself so quickly? She trusted him. Moreover there were mystical connections. (They were to discover more later.) And besides, they looked alike. Both had similarly shaped wide, generous lips, two magnets that had to attract. God, she knew she would kiss him. That is, he would kiss her, for never in a million years would she initiate anything. Their front teeth were angled toward each other, similarly striated and slightly discolored. Both had long lashes and flat, hairy eyebrows that rose up in surprise or astonishment. Their faces were small, oval, with sharp, pointy, slightly upturned goyish noses. And they both had green eyes. When they looked at each other, endless mirrors reflected. Want more? More mystical links? Here's more. His initials were on her license place, she told him. And even more uncanny, both realized something about their phone numbers. She knew it, but he said it first. Happy as a child, he told her that except for one digit, their phone numbers were exactly the same. (He had hers from a registrar's list.) But she contradicted him. No, she said, they are exactly the same. Not the same order, of course, but the numbers were the same. How do you know? Isaac asked, green eyes laughing. She admitted she had called Brookline information to get his home number, not that she would ever have called him. Again, it was something a high school girl with a crush would have done. He pulled out a piece of paper, wrote both numbers, crossed digits out one by one and, behold, conceded she was right. They were anagrammed into each others' phone numbers, and he was monogrammed onto her license plate.

Their first walks were so demure. So exciting. Yes, she trusted him. He seemed a friend. She had always wanted a male friend. One you could share everything with. How great! She could be secretly attracted to him, and they would still be friends. She could daydream and night-dream about him, but her vows would remain intact and her guilt would melt away. It'd be great and safe. Besides, he was probably married.

"How did you know?" he asked. Now he opened his eyes.

"Oh, so you are *paying attention. No, not me. It's not how* I *know. It's her. The Rebecca I'm telling you about. She just assumed he was married."*

No, she decided. He was divorced. All writers were. She'd find out. She was good at looking things up. But she'd have to inquire in a way so as not to let him know she was interested. Do you have children? What a stupid question! That still doesn't answer whether or not he's married.

Maybe he's just being nice, went through Rebecca's head during those lonely days between her Friday classes and Monday. He sees I'm in pain and he wants to help. He knows I'm lonely and unhappy. Yes, that's it—he's being nice. But yet the way he looks directly into her eyes. Each look from his eyes was like a shooting cluster of chartreuse photons, a little bundle of lime-colored light. As if penetrating her insides. Like the questions Isaac asks and his sharp insights into her problems. One remark of his cut through all the obfuscations that she had in two-three years of therapy. Bull's eye. And the way he patted the grass first time they walked in the park—

* * *

"Where'd you pull 'obfuscations' from? And 'chartreuse photons'? Send a girl to college and right away she starts spouting five-dollar words. And, for your information, that pat on the grass was otherspeak for a pat on your . . ."

—telling her to sit down. For days she replayed that pat on the grass as a tender embrace. And the way he lifted up her sunglasses, saying he wanted to see her eyes. And the way he flicked back a lock of her hair from her eyes when her head was down and she was almost in tears, talking about her estrangement from her disturbed mother. He did it like a brother. A friend. The way it might have been done in the movies or on TV. And yet—maybe, could it be because he liked her?

How she looked forward to those Wednesday walks and how she dreaded them. With each walk, each glance, each word spoken she felt closer to him and the attraction wrapped itself round her like ivy round a tree. A new source of conflict she had never anticipated, but yet there it was, present and growing.

Listen, now the good part is coming. The first two times they met they sat facing each other. The third or fourth time they sat very close, shoulders touching. It was then that he asked if she would like to join him for a Pirandello matinee at the Harvard Theater. A month ago she would have thought Pirandello was Italian for a type of pasta. But now, big shot that she was, she was reading *Six Characters in Search of an Author*, one character of which was her, in search of a playwright.

"Spell playright."

"No."

Sure, she said at once without even thinking. A matinee

sounded safe enough. It was during the day, not really a date. Consider it a literary exercise, an assignment for class, for they had just finished reading that play. And, by the way, he never did take her to see that play, or any other for that matter. She's still waiting. Then he got up, said, Let's walk, and stretched his hand out to help her up. She took it, but he didn't let go. And so they walked for twenty or more paces holding hands and the, oh, God, next step, that sweet dreamy step up the ladder, he put his arm around her and she, again without thinking, did the same to him.

She was excited, delirious, floating on air. Rebecca, that is. She still considered all this friendly, brotherly-sisterly, did the very married Rebecca. The next time they met before class and Isaac said, oh so casually, Next time we go to the Lookout wouldn't a picnic be a good idea? And she responded, You know that's exactly what I was going to suggest to you. Can you arrange a Saturday noon? he asked. Perfect, she said, thinking: My husband goes bowling with the guys. And then he winked at her before class began. No one else was in the room, maybe another student who was reading a newspaper. And after class she walked out quickly because she had to go to the bathroom and she saw the disappointed look on his face. What? Rebecca's not going to stay to make arrangements for the picnic? And she mouthed, I'll be right back, so intimately, so secretively, and his face brightened. When she returned, she said, I'll meet you at the Lookout on Saturday at 1 p.m. But we're still going to the park today, right?

Later, in the park, walking side by side, he suddenly took her shoulders, turned her to him and kissed her. She wondered if he had heard that sighed "Oh" that came out of her lips.

As soon as his lips touched hers, she at once excitedly opened her mouth and she knew, oh she knew what would happen next.

Nothing in the world could stop them. Not words. Not don'ts. Not promises. Not vows. Nothing.

Oh yes, the picnic. Let's not forget that Saturday picnic. She had to prepare it at home after hubby left. He was normally dawdly but today frustratingly so. When he finally left with his bowling bag, she ran out to buy a beautiful paper tablecloth, matching paper plates, even a flower in a small vase. She saw Isaac was surprised, pleased, even touched, at the care she took in the presentation. Little did he know that she had almost chickened out. A picnic is an intimate thing, after which she would be on a roller coaster she'd never be able to reverse.

"You're kidding! You never told me that! You almost changed your mind?"

Amy nodded. "You don't know how close I was to not coming."

They sat under a tree, unobserved, minutes from the Lookout, continents away. He lay on his back and she sat on top of him. You can do anything you want to me except fuck me, she said. The crassness of her language startled him, but for someone—and these are Isaac's words—who thought a Pirandello was an Italian pasta, he shouldn't have been surprised. In reply, he slowly put both hands on her breasts and let them rest there for a while, then pressed the palm of his hand to her crotch, as if staking out his territory, signaling what was his. Although Rebecca meant what she said, deep down she knew it was only talk and that his gestures were truer than her words, for she was making love to him in her daydreams every day and what was she doing now, sitting on him and rocking back and forth, if not proxy screwing? Do you know why I like you? he told her. Because you look like me! When I kiss you, I feel like I'm kissing myself. But of course he was joking. After he touched her, a pleasant dreamy weakness filled her like an elixir. If she were standing she would have fallen down. You're gorgeous, she told him, and in her eyes there was what he called a magical look. Describe it, she commanded. It's a look I'll never forget, he said. Describe it, she repeated. She knew there was a hard edge to her challenge. Make me see that look. He closed his eyes, thought for a moment. It's a special aureole, he began slowly. A lime-colored light, a shooting cluster of chartreuse photons . . .

"So that's where you got 'lime-colored light' from, you plagiarist. I thought it sounded familiar!"

. . . a beam that comes from the heart, the mind, the soul, the guts, the gonads, the wings, the footlights, and converges in the eyes where a special bright, radiant little green light shines and says, I want you, I want you, I love you.

I hope that someday I'll see that look in someone's eyes, she said.

Open your eyes and see it, he said.

And then she took his forearm and slowly kissed it from the fingertips to the shoulder.

I still can't believe it, he said, and kissed her again. She had soft, red, perfectly shaped lips, he said. I still can't believe it. Into the classroom walks this gorgeous creature . . .

Her eyes glowed.

. . . and all the girls look up at him ga-ga eyed.

Exactly one month after their first walk—she kept a secret diary with all the important landmarks: first walk, first hand hold, first kiss—they made love. It was all so wonderful and also so scary, Rebecca thought. By then he too had opened up, after first being irritatingly coy and protective about himself. He had been divorced once, was married now, but his wife was teaching political science in San Francisco and they wouldn't see each other until the Christmas break. (Why he would take a job for a year away from his wife she didn't ask but should have.)

Time with him passed so quickly. An hour was like a minute. She was never bored. Long ago, probably after their first kiss, he told her: Between us sparks are going to fly. He was right, but it was an understatement. It was more like fireworks.

Thinking of him affected her at home too. She would become incensed at her poor husband because he wasn't the teacher. He didn't have his spark, his panache. Why couldn't he bring out these feelings in me? Rebecca thought. Our lives would be so perfect.

But she knew why. She didn't, couldn't, love him.

But he, the other he in her life, how possessive he was. As if he'd known her for years. At the beginning, before they even touched, before their demure second walk, he had told her something. Standing by the door of the classroom on a Monday, she was the last to leave, as usual, he said: I know something about you. What? she asked. You smile with your mouth, not with your eyes. Then a few days later, Isaac told her, You know what I'm going to do to you? *To* you, mind you, not for you—and all kinds of puzzling thoughts ran through her head, because what kind of cocky, arrogant statement was that? Then, looking arrow-straight into her eyes, as he always did, he said, I'm going to make your eyes smile. A week later he asked, What if I'd said instead of make your eyes smile, What if I'd said, You know what I'm going to do to you. I'm going to screw you. What if I'd said that? And she said, I was so astonished, so confused, so dumbfounded by the question, it wouldn't have made any difference what you added. You could have said, Turn you into blue cheese, and I wouldn't have heard.

But she also found herself becoming angry with the teacher. She had come to him a drowning soul, looking at college as a lifesaver, a rescue raft, to provide some stability. But now she was more at sea than ever. Now her life was more complicated than before. Had he taken advantage of her honesty and vulnerabilities, making her dependent upon him for the sustenance of her being?

"Sure sounds that way," he interrupts.

Or did she, strong as steel, set her sights on what she wanted and would later conquer? After all, she was reputed to be the strong one in the family, taking care of finances, paying bills, managing vacations. The pants wearer in the family, while goyish hubby did his plodding supervisor's work for the Boston Welfare Department.

"But your pants are on backwards!"

"Don't mock. It's painful and you're making light of it. You know, you're more sensitive as a teacher than you are as a real man."

Anyway, she was smitten. In love. Head over—wanna hear another cliché?—heels. The indescribable love of a woman for a man, that delicate honey of the sweetest nectar. She couldn't sleep. Only think of him. Oh, God, if one could only bottle those first six weeks of love. That magic. That bliss. And lovemaking was ecstatic. Clichés fell into place like dominoes toppling.

"Cli—," he said. "No. I take that back. That's rather imaginative!"

* * *

She felt her heart pounding. Her breathing became heavy. Her body pulsating.

"Three clichés in a row. You're out."

"Enough! Listen to the message. Not the words."

You're just one big sexual being, she told him. You're sexy all over. Everything about you, from your eyes down, radiates sexuality.

"My God, you remember everything. You don't forget a word."

"I'm not like you. You forget half the things you say."

"That still means I'm batting .500. That's great in any league, but you didn't say all that at once. Those are phrases you used over the months."

"Listen to the message. Not the words."

Rebecca was alive. This was love. She had felt it only once before, as a teenager. But now as an adult it was different. More intense. More real. There were no inhibitions. No pretensions. She was able to be herself. She felt total abandon.

"Only one syllable, Amy, separates abandon from abandoned. Even less."

"Don't I know it!"

Anyway, it was total abandon.

She remembers the first time he said to her, You look like Judy Garland. And she said, Thanks. To which he said, It's not meant to be a compliment. I was sort of pleased with that quirky insult. But when I saw it in one of your plays I realized it wasn't me you were saying it to but one of your characters. You used me as a sounding board for your wit. And then I began to wonder if you meant, or didn't mean, anything you said to me. Because for you—the play's the thing.

"I didn't write: It's not meant to be a compliment. I wrote: It's not meant as a compliment."

"Why?"

"Saved a syllable. Sounds crisper. But you still look like Judy Garland."

"Is that a compliment?"

"Now it is."

"Where am I gonna read that?"

"Have patience."

"The logo of my life."

And he too was in love, he claimed. But he doesn't know what love is. He's ready to throw it away. She knew that. For as much as she knew about him there was one more thing she knew. She knew it wouldn't, couldn't, last. No. Not with him. With him nothing could be forever. That's why she wanted him to finish the story for her.

Why doesn't he want her? Is he ashamed of her? Because she's not as smart as him? Because he thinks of her as a cultural Neanderthal? I know, I know, that's your term too. So what if I didn't start reading 'til recently. Or if I don't know anything about music or art. Some people get a late start in life. Does that diminish their worth? Or doesn't he want her because of her mother's mental illness? Would he be ashamed to take her to an intellectual party? Arthur Miller wasn't ashamed of Marilyn Monroe.

* * *

"He wasn't ashamed of Joe DiMaggio either!"

And another thing. How could something that is so sweet, so pure, be so wrong? she thought. There was a saying: You can't go back. Maybe it's a cliché, but so what? You can only move forward. So many times she tried to end this "affair." Why had she opened this Pandora's box?

"The teacher opened Pandora's box too."

"But not for the first time," she said nastily.

"Very funny," he says.

She can hear the downspin in his voice. She's gotten to him. And glad of it.

She had had secret crushes on other men. But they never picked up the signals. She knew that she would never let things get out of hand. Or did she not send the signals clearly? In any case, she had never bared her soul—

"Or her ass," he says flippantly.

"See? That's the difference between me and you. Between women and men. I take emotions seriously."

—with such total nakedness as she had for him. And it seemed so easy, so fluid, so natural.

Why? What possessed her to allow this to happen? She'd never even told people she'd known for years anything about herself. Like how she'd been beaten as a child. Then why such quick and open honesty with him? Because she likes him and didn't care what he thought of her. It didn't matter.

Confusion, anger, resolution. These emotions would well

up inside her and violently pound in her mind like stormy seas—

"Cliché!"

—over and over again. And yet there is nothing more beautiful or tender than lying in his arms after wildly passionate love-making, she thought.

But it's wrong.

She wants to be a good Jew. Like the grandfathers and grand-mothers from the Old World in the teacher's plays. Some Jew she's turned out to be. Instead of adding some new mitzvas to her nonexistent Jewish repertoire, she had sacrificed the Seventh Commandment. Just like her abusive mother before her had done. Perhaps it was genetic. And if she ever had children, would they betray their husbands too? Then again, according to Jewish law she's not a married woman. She married a non-Jew. So technically, she's not committing adultery. But Isaac—he's married.

"Will you please look a little more focused when I'm telling you a story?"

"Only clichés perk me up."

They gorge themselves with physical pleasure—a symphony of eroticism. Yet do they take time to consider their sins against their spouses and against God?

What should they do? Deny the reality that has existed, is in existence, and will exist as long as they live? Perhaps they were fated to be lovers, just like their phone numbers had exactly the same digits and his initials were on her license plate, perhaps it was fated that their lives run their course until the inevitable was to happen and *que sera sera*—

* * *

"Cliché!"

"I don't care Okay, I've told you the story, sweetie. Now it's your turn. The curtain's up. The house lights are off. The audience is waiting. For the playwright to speak. What's going to happen next? Spotlight's on you, pussycat. End it for me. Tell me what's going to happen. Tell me what became of this woman and the man who stirred the depths of her soul and mind, her heart and body? What's next for Isaac and Rebecca? What's going to be? Finish this story. Please. Finish the play Let's have the third act."

"First kiss me. More . . . more . . . Is that the end?"

"End of what? The kissing you or the story?"

"The end of the story."

"There is no end. That's it. What I told you. Now you finish. I told you the beginning. Now tell me the end."

He shrugged. "How can I finish another person's story?"

"Because it's your story too, Isaac."

He was silent.

"Well, say something. Anything! Remember you once poked fun at Rebecca when she was considering leaving her husband and had told her teacher that she was sort of hesitant to do it because: I have to have my clothing and a roof over my head. And you couldn't stop laughing at me putting my clothing before the roof. But never mind, that's not important now. What's more important is the ending. Finish this story. Okay, you're silent. But I'm not letting you off the hook, Isaac. Just giving you a breather. To think a bit. I won't let you remain silent much longer. You're going to speak. You're going to become more than a cliché-cruncher. You're going to finish this story. You must. The play's the thing. The audience demands the ending."

Actually, Rebecca has come to understand that there is no

ending. Just as there was no beginning. That which will happen has already been written—like the Book that God inscribes at the beginning of the Jewish New Year. There are no erasures or additions. Just as if what has happened cannot be deleted. Yes, it can be denied to others. But these two lovers cannot deny that which has already connected their bodies and souls forever. For she remembered what Rebecca, the Biblical one, not the heroine, had said to Eliezer before his search for Isaac. No, you won't find it in the Bible. It's a Midrashic legend, a kind of mirror image to the actual Biblical story. See? I looked that up too, just like I looked up all your plays and TV scripts. Rebecca said to Eliezer: When you have found the possessor of the traits I seek, good heart, great mind, poetic soul, goodly of visage and form, bring him forth, for he shall be mine for all eternity.

"Now finish this story for me, will you, sweetie?"

"I can't give you the ending. There's so many endings in life."

"Well, think about it, because I'm not finished yet. You see, Rebecca feels guilty about what she's been doing. She's so confused and sad."

"Remember what I once said: I'm going to make your eyes smile?"

That's all very well and good, but Rebecca doesn't want to be on the periphery of his life. She wants to be in the center. She's greedy. But he's content to see her only once in a while, while she falls into a depression every time she leaves him, so she feels it's better not to see him at all because she loves him too much and loving a man like him too much is no good. She gives him too much of herself while he holds back, is careful and silent. He's content to see her when he wants to see her. And she wants to become less emotionally dependent on him. Loving a man too much in marriage is fine but not in a secret affair. And Rebecca's husband—your eyes are closed again, Isaac. Are you tuning out?

"Cliché!" he said.

Her husband, who hasn't paid much attention to her, and with whom she's had an on-again, off-again marriage and for whom she feels a friendship but not love, wants to get closer to her now that he senses her drifting away. And what would she say if she ever had children and they find out about her behavior and lose respect for her the way she lost respect for her unstable mother? It's a miracle you turned out the way you did, so good and loving, Isaac had told her, because abused children are all screwed up.

Okay. Now you can talk. Now I'm done. So what's the ending? What do you think? You're so smart, what's the ending? What's going to be? Finish the story!

"Relax! You sound hysterical. Get that hyper edge out of your voice. You expect resolution now?"

"Yes! Now!"

"What is this, a playwriting course?"

"I want an ending. Closure."

"There could be lots of endings."

"Just give me one. One? Please?"

"I'm not God."

"Very modest of you. But give me one anyway. Just one, for goodness sake!"

"There's never only one ending in life. That's only for the movies. There's lots . . ."

"One. Give me one. One. Come on! Let me hear it. Just one."

"Calm down. My God, you sound so . . . Come on, it's not

like you. One could be the Hollywood ending. One the O. Henry. One could be the French cinema verité."

"What's the Hollywood?"

"The moral one. From the '40s. Each goes back to their respective spouse to their respectable house and lives happily ever after . . ."

"Cliché,"Amy shouts.

". . . like a mouse. Or in the 1970s Hollywood version: unhappily. The O. Henry ending is that here is no ending. Or like the story, 'The Lady or the Tiger?' the author leaves it up to the reader. Your husband gets the lady or you get the tiger. Or maybe not the lady or the tiger, but a tiger lady like you. Or maybe even a tiger lady without teeth."

"Like you," she said.

"But with balls. Better no teeth than no balls."

"My paper tiger," she said. "And the French verité ending?"

"That's a good one. The guy goes to the girl's house under some pretext and falls for the husband and the two fellows hit it off. Or the guy—this is the nineteenth-century grand novel ending—could run off with the girl. And then for all that there are two possibilities. They could either be happy or unhappy. Probably unhappy because if you run off, you leave behind the two most important assets in life: your clothing and your roof. Or the guy could knock on the husband's door with the full intent of declaring his love for his wife and, in a Chekhovian twist, see the sorrow in the man's eyes, the emptiness of his house, and suddenly his resolve deflates, detumesces like a frightened rooster—the woman is meanwhile exchanging hysterical glances with him—and he, the sudden wimp, says he's selling life insurance. Or the two couples could meet and the affairs crisscross—that's the Italian cinema ending with a Scandinavian flavor, with a twist of Helsinki, let's call it a photo

Finnish. And still another ending could be the flat-out cable TV version where all four meet at a restaurant but they have to use plastic forks . . ."

"Why?"

"So they shouldn't kill each other. My God, I told you there's heaps and heaps of endings. The two women could hit it off. Or softcore porn, all four make it with the middle-aged divorced waitress."

"Will you give me just one?"

"Okay, each of the four runs off with . . . the menu."

"You're hopeless. Come on! You're so imaginative. Give me one ending. Finish this story. I'm so confused I don't know what to do. Give me an ending, please. I'm so sad," she whispered. "I could . . ." and she drifted off.

"Beginnings are easy. Continuations are easier. It's the endings that are hard. You know what? I got the perfect answer."

"What?"

"Since you asked the questions, why don't you create an ending?"

"I did," Amy said a week later.

"Did what?" he asked.

"You forgot?"

"No. Forgot what?"

"You are hopeless. I created an ending for Rebecca's story. In the seven days since I saw you last I've thought of nothing else. Here it is. It's called 'The Story's End: A Harlequin Romance.'"

Plagued with guilt, the lovers return to their spouses, houses, and mouses—initially with renewed enthusiasm, the sparks and sparkle left over from each other, and the hope for a brighter future with partners with whom they share a history. For what history do Rebecca and her love, Isaac, share with each other? One love, two lives. Everything secret.

A woman in love radiates a certain beauty—a glow—she carries herself differently, confidently. She glides as though she's walking on air, above the ground. Like those hi-tech trains they have in Japan and France.

"How about a natural image, a bird or something, the way a woman—not a man—thinks and feels?"

How she longed to go to public places with him. To do the things that lovers do in the summertime. Strolling down Fifth Avenue on a Sunday afternoon, waking up with him after a Saturday night of passion and play to luxuriate in bed on Sunday morning. Picnics in the park. Afternoons of leisure. How she longed never to have to worry about time or responsibility. Well, this was all fantasy, because she's back with the husband, he's with his wife.

"Hey that's my Hollywood ending, either Number One or Number Two."

"Shh! This is a Harlequin Romance, sweetie, wait for the plot to develop."

They continue their lives as they once were, trying to make the best of each day, week, month, and year. Years go by. The fires that were once an integral part of her love for him have all but died down. She will never forget him, but she has to get on with the functions of her existence.

"Cliché!"

"It's not a cliché. Get on with her life is a cliché. And don't interrupt."

* * *

—and he has to get on with his. She can't speak for him, because she was never really sure how he felt. He used words like "darling" and "lovely"—but they were only words, words he would ply, ploy, play her with, thinking she needed to hear them. That's not what she needed. He never did feel, never will feel for her what she felt for him.

"How do you know?"

"I know. Because deeds count, Isaac Gelber, not words. And don't interrupt again."

Part of her was crushed by this reality, but part of her didn't care. But on with the story. She went back to the husband, continued studying, and in her mid-forties became a successful and attractive—

"I'm sorry. I must interrupt. What do you mean 'became attractive'? Wasn't Rebecca beautiful now, and always? You told me once that you were Miss White Plains. You're making it sound as if she'd undergone some chic Salon Transformation, the poor Cinderella."

"She became even more attractive."

—a successful and attractive attorney. She became even more attractive. The years ripened and deepened her beauty.

"The judges in the courtroom had to install special drooling cups to drool into when she appeared in court. They would get tongue-tied. One judge, looking at her, sentenced a criminal to 'sex years in the clinker'. . ."

* * *

She had never allowed another affair to happen and was able to concentrate on her work, and with the husband—they had no children—she had a cool and correct relationship. A marriage of convenience. Reading Isaac's plays had an effect on her. She always remembered his influence. And so the fires were replaced with a shining light, always allowing her to see things in a new and different fashion. Her instincts had always been sharp, but now she was less critical of herself and of others than she had been when she was younger.

He went back to the wife, but after a year-and-a-half they were separated and finally divorced. He had had many affairs, but nothing with substance because that's not what he wanted, just superficial sexual encounters to satisfy his superego. He was prolific and by now famous and very successful. Many of his plays had been turned into movies and he had been nominated for the Pulitzer Prize. He still continued to teach at Brandeis, where he had once guest lectured. Was it because he wanted to be near the girl he had loved that he gave up his West Coast roots? Who knows? By this time he had pretty much forgotten about Rebecca. He had women throwing themselves at him and was leading a life of physical and moral depravity. He was happy.

"Moral and physical depravity and happy? What a queer combo! Absolutely unrealistic. I pity the poor shmo."

"I told you it's a Harlequin Romance," Amy said. "Meanwhile, Rebecca's husband had died."

"You mean dried. He just desiccated away, little by little, until she put him into a little Ziploc bag and dropped the now tiny goy in the local parish graveyard."

* * *

As I was saying, Rebecca's husband died when she was in her mid-forties. She was very successful in her career. Now she thought often about the teacher, the playwright, the playboy, the only man she had ever loved. How she loved that man. She had given herself to him so easily. Had she had a chance she would have done it all differently. How he didn't appreciate what he had! How we don't appreciate those people who love us, despite all our faults and shortcomings, and how we yearn for those we never had. If she were to do it over, she wouldn't have loved him so easily, so freely. He would have wanted her more. That's how men are. It's too difficult to explain—a story in itself.

"Cliché! Not the words. The thought. Who says so? It's backtrack thinking. And if she hadn't *given in so easily? And what does* that *mean? Screwing him on the sixth, not the third meeting? People do what they want to do. It's only when things don't work out for them that they blame themselves for their actions and create roads at a fork, the road not chosen being the better one, of course. Had things worked out she'd be patting herself on the back for her wise course of conduct. And don't roll your beautiful green eyes, it's making me dizzy. Finish this story."*

Because of her expertise in the field of legal ethics, she was invited to give a series of lectures at Brandeis, the school she had attended long ago. She had always loved the place from the first day she set foot in it. The country atmosphere, the woods, the lake, the whole setting. But she realized it was only because she had met him there that very first day of her college career. Oh, the memories it held for her. Meeting him at her very first class of her very first day of college. And now, the months before her first lecture seemed like an eternity. Would he be there? Would he read the publicity flyer announcing her coming? Would she see him? Would she dare look him up? Call him? The truth is, she did want to see him. She had to tell him something; show him something. Something she had kept from him when they broke up, abruptly, more than fifteen years ago. His latest play, the one that was being filmed, was actually a thinly disguised retelling of their affair and of a play outline she'd written for his class. And he hadn't even acknowledged her! Instead, in the program, he had written a lovely letter of dedication to his ex-wife. They were divorced and he was dedicating the play, her play, her life, to his ex-wife! Women always brought out the wimp in him. He even used to hunch his back and mumble when his wife's name was mentioned. And she was three thousand miles away. Imagine what he'd look like if his wife had been in town? I even heard that he had to see a speech pathologist because she caused him to stutter and this interfered with his teaching. Could there ever be a more respectable, upstanding human being in the whole wide world than him?!

"Sarcastic, nasty, catty woman lawyer," Isaac interjected.

Although at one time the now attractive and successful attorney would have counted her losses and shrugged it off, now she was ready to deal with him as an academic equal. She would confront him. But what did she want, money? No, not really—she was wealthier than she ever imagined she would be. Did she want revenge because he had disposed of her so easily? No, actually she was still in love with him and all she wanted was for him to love her. But she knew this would never happen. This is where the real anger came from. Yes. She would confront him.

Four months passed and she began her series of Brandeis lectures on law and ethics. At the first lecture, heart pounding, she looked for him, but he wasn't in the small auditorium, the one in which she'd sat in the first row for his playwriting class years ago. Again, after all these years, that secret thrill, like a bittersweet perfume, missing seeing his face. But maybe he was out of town, giving his own lecture somewhere or watching a rehearsal of a new play. How she longed to share her glory, the spotlight he had always had. To have his respect and to see her as something more than a pretty sexual toy. But after her second lecture, as she walked to her car, she saw a man approaching. He walked toward her with a faintly recognizable gait. Yes, it was him, lithe and agile as always. His face, while handsome, was different. It was his eyes. They no longer danced. That leap of green light was gone. His mouth was smiling (had he recognized her?) and polite words came out, but his eyes were flat and empty. Those beautiful green laughing eyes she had once loved, had the fire gone out of them? And there were flecks of gray in his formerly black curly hair.

"Hi, how are you?" he said shyly. For a moment he looked straight into her eyes as he had years ago, but then he looked past her, as if staring out at the horizon. It seemed as if he didn't want to, couldn't look into her eyes. But perhaps he was just looking at her hair. "I heard you were coming," he said. "Sorry I missed your first talk. I was away. But I heard this one and it was great."

"I didn't see you."

"I purposely sat in the back. I thought if you saw me you might get flustered."

"The ego is still large."

"And your voice still is like beige velvet. And you still have those gorgeous green eyes. Deeper, lovelier than ever. I thought I would have heard from you sooner."

He tried to charm her with words; how easily it would work for him more than fifteen years ago.

She didn't smile. Yes, she still loved him, but she wouldn't allow him to charm her with his sly grin and golden words as she had at an earlier time in her life. She confronted him with his play and told him it was a verbatim account of their affair and of a play she had written for his course. Did he do that with all his students? Assign assignments and then plagiarize their writing? Of all people, how could he have done this to her?

"I changed things. Disguised them. To protect you. Your husband . . ."

"Ex-," she said tartly.

". . . would never have noticed. I made everything different. I never called you Miss White Plains. I said I heard you on the radio for something or other. I forget."

"That's your trouble, you forget."

He was about to say something but she added:

"And that dedication to your wife—"

"Ex-"

"—that really takes the cake. I found it disgusting."

"Oho! Little Miss Muffet is miffed. I purposely did that. For you. To protect you. So that no one should know. And if you read it carefully, you'll see how sensitive I was to all the details let's not argue okay? Now? Now to argue, at first seeing after all these years? Look, can you wait here for a little bit? I'm expecting a call at the office in a couple of minutes. The National Theatre of London. Five, maximum ten minutes, then I want to show you something."

"I don't have time. I have to get back to my office." Oh how proud she was to say that. How she dreamt years ago of uttering a line like that.

"Never mind. I changed my mind. The National Theatre can

wait. If they want me they'll call again. I'm not going back to my office." He took her hand. "Come. Get in the car. I must show you something."

She couldn't resist. As soon as he touched her the fifteen-plus years vanished. Those forearms. How she loved those forearms of his. She would always tell him how much she loved his arms and his legs and his eyes and his . . . She got in the car. Felt that ever-burning eternal light burst into flame for him. The flame she used to feel. She watched him as he drove. A two-seater sports car. A Lamborghini, no less, one of the world's most expensive. Here was the same man with the same self-confident look. But he was different. Changed. Mellowed?

They drove for about half an hour, into the north country. Farms and fields, a rural area, the same back roads they would travel together. He didn't say much. He didn't ask about her practice. He didn't wonder why she had to go back to her office. He didn't apologize for taking her away from her work. He didn't ask if she had remarried. He didn't make any lawyer jokes. He hadn't changed. Just once in a while he ordered her, "Look at me, not the road," like he used to years back.

At one point during the silence she burst out with: I love that line in your play where the guy says to the girl, I'm looking forward to seeing you again, and the girl says, Likewise. And the guy says, I don't mean what I'm saying, do you? And the girl says, No. The audience laughed its head off. That joke is so, I mean, it's so you. And he laughed too, pleased, as if she'd come up with the joke.

They turned into a dirt road lined with trees that ascended and curved. He stopped in front of the gate of a large estate. The property had a beautiful garden and well-manicured lawn, all away from the public view, absolutely private.

"So," she said, "what do you want to show me? This? I've been to Europe. I've seen castles. Am I supposed to be impressed?" He looked at her, oblivious to her sarcasm, and smiled. Slowly, life came into his eyes. Now, for the first time, they were laughing.

He got out of the car.

"Let's go in," he said.

"Why?"

"No why," he said.

At the door he picked her up. She was as slim and light as she'd been in her late twenties. "You haven't changed. You still look great. Beautiful." And then he added slowly. "Lovely."

She said nothing. But she had to put her arms around his neck so as to not fall down.

"You're supposed to say, and so do you," he said.

He opened the door not with a key but with a code and carried her into the house. It all became one blur to her. Paintings and mirrors, Persian carpets, sculptures, antiques. She had no idea where she was or why they were in this splendidly appointed mansion. After all, they had spent most of their time together in a musty, dingy apartment—the best time of her life. And now he was showing her the tangibles of his success.

He carried her up the winding staircase to a large room. As soon as they crossed the threshold she was dumbfounded. The room, down to the last detail, was a clone of the one she had once fantasized, one in which she'd wanted to be with him years ago. The room she had imagined they would make love in for the first time. And he had remembered. He had said that important things he did not forget. He's remembered every word: the cherry Victorian furniture, the Louis XIV poster bed, the blue Delft porcelain water pitcher and bowl, even the pink roses in the Waterford vase. Exactly as she had daydreamed it. And she knew that in the bath, which would be large with a sunken tub, there would be a peach-colored candle set at the rim.

"So you really were listening to me back then."

"To every word. To everything you said." He held her shoulders, brought his face close to hers. Held her face. The fire of his green eyes singed her. "You're right. I should have acknowledged your contribution to my play, our play. It would have been the right thing to do."

"Even the legal and ethical," she quipped.

"Instead, I bought this house for—" he paused—"us. You see, here's . . ." and he went to an antique cherrywood highboy and opened a drawer. "See? Here's the deed. It's in your name too."

"You mean—"

"Yes." He didn't let her finish the sentence. But then he said, "What? Finish the sentence."

"I forgot what I was going to say," she said.

Well, although she never understood him, and would never understand why she didn't understand him, she knew that that wasn't important. She loved him and, finally, after all these years, knew that he loved her too.

"And I have a little surprise for you too," she said, smiling. She opened her purse and took out a picture of a handsome green-eyed adolescent.

"This is Jeremy. Your son. The picture was taken when he became Bar Mitzvah two years ago . . ."

"I've finished the story."

"Wow!" he said. "What an ending! You know you will have that room some day."

Amy closed her eyes, savoring the word. It's not the room she wants, she says aloud. Think about what I want. I want you. She doesn't want anything glitzy from him. With him pizza is as good as caviar. She wants to acquire life's tangibles on her own. But there is one thing she can't provide herself with. She thought she had found it, but isn't quite sure now. His reactions to her have been startling. Shattering realities have slapped her in the face and woken her up to the real world. She's no longer content flitting around aimlessly like a butterfly, blowing in whichever direction the wind carries her—a thing of beauty that won't last forever, only to end up matted and framed and hung up on someone's mantle—with a pin through her midsection.

She would have that room some day, she hears him promise. She wants to believe those words but knows not to. Were they still in that Harlequin Romance world?

Isaac held her face.

"You're gonna publish this. I know it. If you publish it, will I get credit?"

"Of course," he said. "And in your honor I'll call the story, 'Amy Says: Finish This Story.'"

"Really?"

"Absolutely."

"Promise?"

"I do."

"A promise is not enough. Promises are cheap."

"Well, so am I," Isaac said.

"Stop it."

"Then what do you want me to do?"

"Swear," she said.

"Okay, I swear."

"No. Not enough. I want you to swear like in the Bible. Like Abraham made Eliezer swear."

"Okay."

"Put your hand under my thigh," she said.

"Fine. If one must swear, this is the way to go."

"Mmm! No! Stop it. Keep your fingers still."

"I love Jewish swearing." he said. "Where'd you learn that?"

"Be serious. Now say . . . I swear . . . Don't . . . Stop moving your hand."

"I swear I won't stop moving my hand."

"Enough, Isaac. Now repeat after me: If I publish this story . . ."

"If I publish this story . . ."

"I swear I will call it: 'Amy Says: Finish This Story.' Do you swear?"

"I do. I will. I shall. I swear. I swear that if I publish this story I'll even call it, 'My Gorgeous Divine Amy says: Finish This Story.'"

"Do you really really really swear?"

"I really really really do. I do. I do. I do."

ABOUT THE AUTHOR

Curt Leviant is author of nine critically acclaimed works of fiction. He has won the Edward Lewis Wallant Award and writing fellowships from the National Endowment for the Arts, the Rockefeller Foundation, the Jerusalem Foundation, the Emily Harvey Foundation in Venice, and the New Jersey Arts Council.

His work has been included in *Best American Short Stories, Prize Stories: The O. Henry Awards* and other anthologies, and praised by two Nobel laureates: Saul Bellow and Elie Wiesel. His novels have been translated into French, Italian, Spanish, Greek, and Romanian, among other languages, and some have been international bestsellers. He lives in Brooklyn, NY.

CURT LEVIANT

FROM OPEN ROAD MEDIA

OPEN ROAD
INTEGRATED MEDIA

www.ingramcontent.com/pod-product-compliance
Lightning Source LLC
Chambersburg PA
CBHW031310280626
47169CB00017B/1185

* 9 7 8 1 5 0 4 0 8 0 5 1 4 *